CPS-LASAL  **P9-BZA-186**

3 29101 0903798 8   808.8 WHA
What you wish for : stories

DATE DUE			

3 29101 0903798 8

808.8
WHA

What you wish for :
stories and poems
for Darfur

LASALLE II MAGNET
CHICAGO PUBLIC SCHOOLS
1148 N HONORE
CHICAGO, IL 60622

382361 01259   62873D   0001

WHAT YOU WISH FOR

Stories and Poems for Darfur

WHAT YOU WISH FOR

Stories and Poems for Darfur

Book Wish

G. P. PUTNAM'S SONS

An Imprint of Penguin Group (USA) Inc.

G. P. PUTNAM'S SONS • A DIVISION OF PENGUIN YOUNG READERS GROUP.
Published by The Penguin Group.
Penguin Group (USA) Inc., 375 Hudson Street, New York, NY 10014, U.S.A.
Penguin Group (Canada), 90 Eglinton Avenue East, Suite 700, Toronto, Ontario M4P 2Y3,
Canada (a division of Pearson Penguin Canada Inc.).
Penguin Books Ltd, 80 Strand, London WC2R 0RL, England.
Penguin Ireland, 25 St. Stephen's Green, Dublin 2, Ireland (a division of Penguin Books Ltd.).
Penguin Group (Australia), 250 Camberwell Road, Camberwell, Victoria 3124, Australia
(a division of Pearson Australia Group Pty Ltd).
Penguin Books India Pvt Ltd, 11 Community Centre, Panchsheel Park, New Delhi - 110 017, India.
Penguin Group (NZ), 67 Apollo Drive, Rosedale, Auckland 0632, New Zealand
(a division of Pearson New Zealand Ltd).
Penguin Books (South Africa) (Pty) Ltd, 24 Sturdee Avenue, Rosebank,
Johannesburg 2196, South Africa.
Penguin Books Ltd, Registered Offices: 80 Strand, London WC2R 0RL, England.

Collection copyright © 2011 by Book Wish Foundation.
Foreword copyright © 2011 by Mia Farrow. "The Strange Story of Bobby Box" copyright
© 2011 by Alexander McCall Smith. "Pearl's Fateful Wish" copyright © 2011 by Jeanne DuPrau.
"Wishes" copyright © 2011 by Jane Yolen. "The Protectionist" copyright © 2011 by Meg Cabot.
"The Great Wall" copyright © 2011 by Sofia Quintero. "Nell" copyright © 2011 by Karen Hesse.
"What I Wish For" copyright © 2011 by Gary Soto. "Reasons" copyright © 2011 by John Green.
"The Lost Art of Letter Writing" copyright © 2011 by Ann M. Martin. "Secret Song" copyright
© 2011 by Naomi Shihab Nye. "The Stepsister" copyright © 2011 by Cynthia Voigt. "Rosanna"
copyright © 2004, 2011 by Cornelia Funke. Originally published by Verlag Friedrich Oetinger,
Germany, 2004, with illustrations by Jackie Gleich. "I Wish I Could Live (In A Book)" copyright
© 2011 by Nikki Giovanni. "Funny Things" copyright © 2011 by R. L. Stine. "Cautious
Wishing" copyright © 2011 by Marilyn Nelson. "The Rules for Wishing" copyright © 2011 by
Francisco X. Stork. "Conjurers" copyright © 2011 by Nate Powell. "The Sky Blue Ball" from
Small Avalanches and Other Stories copyright © 2003 by The Ontario Review, Inc.
All rights reserved. This book, or parts thereof, may not be reproduced in any form without
permission in writing from the publisher, G. P. Putnam's Sons, a division of Penguin Young
Readers Group, 345 Hudson Street, New York, NY 10014.
G. P. Putnam's Sons, Reg. U.S. Pat. & Tm. Off. The scanning, uploading and distribution of this
book via the Internet or via any other means without the permission of the publisher is illegal and
punishable by law. Please purchase only authorized electronic editions, and do not participate
in or encourage electronic piracy of copyrighted materials. Your support of the author's rights is
appreciated. The publisher does not have any control over and does not assume any responsibility
for author or third-party websites or their content.
Published simultaneously in Canada. Printed in the United States of America.
Design by Marikka Tamura. Text set in Stempel Garamond.
Library of Congress Cataloging-in-Publication Data is available upon request.

ISBN 978-0-399-25454-3
3 5 7 9 10 8 6 4 2

To the more than 250,000 Darfuris
living in refugee camps in Chad.

CONTENTS

"Nothing is more important for children than education. It is the promise of a better future. And nowhere is this more true than in eastern Chad, where education helps protect against risks ranging from early marriage to recruitment into armed forces. The authors of this book have generously given the gift of their stories to help create a better and more hopeful world for these young people. By reading them, you are doing the same. Thank you."

—ANTÓNIO GUTERRES,
UN High Commissioner for Refugees

FOREWORD

Since 2004, I have made thirteen journeys into the Chad/Darfur region. I have friends in refugee camps across eastern Chad. Whenever I visit, the kids swarm around me, shyly chanting my name as they pull me toward their tents or huts, where I sit on the mat and their mother serves thick, sugary tea. We communicate in a blend of (very) elementary Arabic, French, gales of laughter and improvised sign language. But there is always at least one kid who will eventually appear and be able to speak all those languages—and sometimes English too.

Mohammed is just such a boy. For almost eight years he has lived in Djabal refugee camp with his older brother. The boys had been tending the family goats when their village was attacked. With their baby sister tied to Mohammed's back, they hid in the brush and watched their village burn. When the baby cried, they covered her mouth. Afterward they searched for their parents but both had been killed. The children joined some other survivors and they walked for nine days—into Chad. The baby did not survive the journey.

Mohammed taught himself to speak then to read English and French by befriending the UNHCR* team and going through wastepaper baskets in the offices. "I want to be a doctor," Mo-

*United Nations High Commissioner for Refugees

hammed told me. "If only I could have a teacher." Pointing to a distant mountain, he said, "I would walk to that mountain and back every day if I could go to secondary school."

Despite his losses, and nearly eight years in a refugee camp with no end in sight, Mohammed's dream is very much alive. And this is the amazing thing; no matter how dire the circumstances or bleak the prospects, every child I have met in Chad, Sudan, the Central African Republic, the Democratic Republic of the Congo, Uganda, or Angola has a dream. Their faces light up when I ask them, "What do you hope to be when you grow up?" "I want to be a doctor, a teacher, a pilot, the president of my country," they shout excitedly. The children long for peace, and even when they don't have enough food, they hunger for a teacher, for books—for the education they know is essential to make their dreams come true.

The stories in this book are about wishes. Just as the first story says, it is never too late for wishes to come true. We can still help the people of Darfur. For refugees worldwide, this year marks the sixtieth anniversary of the United Nations agreement that gives them protection, the Convention Relating to the Status of Refugees. They are still there, hoping, wishing, dreaming—and we can still help.

MIA FARROW
Actor, Advocate,
UNICEF Goodwill Ambassador,
and Mother
January 23, 2011

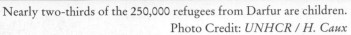
Nearly two-thirds of the 250,000 refugees from Darfur are children.
Photo Credit: *UNHCR / H. Caux*

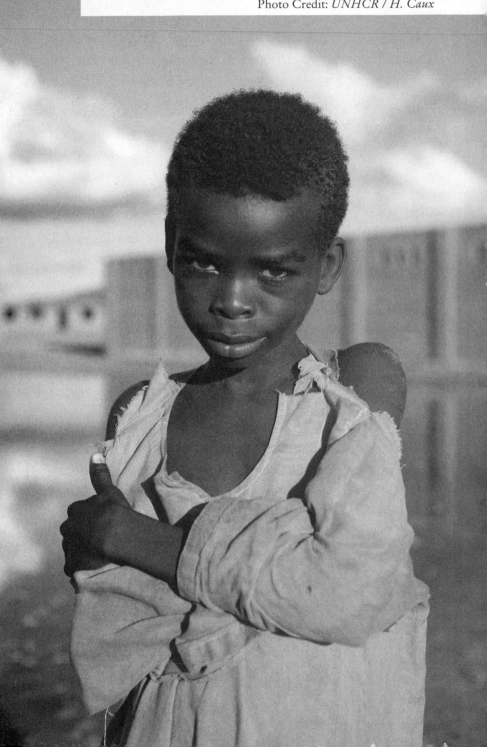

ALEXANDER McCALL SMITH

THE STRANGE STORY OF BOBBY BOX

Have you ever thought of what your life story would sound like if you told it to somebody? Many people would probably say, "Not all that unusual" or "Not very interesting." And maybe that's true—for most of us—but then there are people whose life stories are very different. If they told us what had happened to them, we might think, "This can't be true" or perhaps "You're making it up."

That's what they said to Bobby. They said that he must be making it up—but he wasn't, you know. Everything he said about what happened to him was true—down to the very last detail. And now here's his story.

1

Most life stories begin with parents. So you say something like, "My mother was twenty-five when she had me. She had dark black hair and a lovely smile and . . ." And so on. Bobby could not say this. He never knew his mother, and he never knew his father. This was because he was found in an open-topped wooden box, one used for packing oranges, floating down a river. A fisherman who was rowing his boat upstream saw the box coming down to meet him, moving slowly in the middle of the current. He shipped his oars and waited for the box to draw level with him, and you can imagine his surprise when he saw what it contained. "By all the stars in heaven," he muttered as he reached out to grab the side of the box before it floated past. "By all the stars in heaven—and the moon too!" That may sound like a strange thing to say, but then the sight of a box containing a little baby wrapped up in a white blanket was a rather strange sight.

Taking great care, the fisherman took the baby from the box and laid him down on the bottom of his boat. Then he slipped his oars back into the rowlocks and rowed as fast as he could for the jetty he used, which was just a short distance upstream. Unfortunately he forgot all about the box, which drifted away with the current and was never seen again. This was a mistake, because it might have contained some clue as to who the baby was. There might have been a letter, or perhaps even a note saying something like *This baby is the property of . . .* and then given a name. As it was, there was nothing on the blanket or on the baby's clothes to give any idea of who he was and why he had been put into this tiny vessel, this orange box, and made to float down the river.

"You should have looked," said the policeman to whom the fisherman later reported his extraordinary find. "You should have looked in the box. You were very careless!"

The fisherman defended himself. "What could I do?" he protested. "I had to get the baby into the boat. I couldn't fiddle about with the box as well."

They left it at that, but the policeman was clearly annoyed. Remember that this all took place in a remote part of Scotland, in a place where he was the only policeman for twenty miles or so. Now here he was landed with a baby, of all things, and his wife was away staying with her sister on the island of Skye for a month. How could he be expected to look after this baby?

He told the fisherman to sit down while he wrote an entry in his book. "Time: 2:30 p.m. Lost property brought into station. Nature of lost property: one baby (male). Action: returned to finder for safekeeping."

Satisfied with the entry in his book, he looked at the fisherman and told him what he would have to do. "You found this baby," he said. "You'll have to look after it, I'm afraid."

The fisherman's eyes widened with astonishment. He struggled to find words, and eventually all that he could say was, "What?"

The policeman explained, "We have no room here to keep a baby. And babies require food and . . . and all sorts of things. You found this baby—you look after him. Sorry about that, but that's the law."

The fisherman knew little about the law—in fact, he knew nothing about it. And in those days, when a policeman told you that the law said this or that, you believed him. So he picked up the baby and took him home to the small cottage that he had on the edge of the bay. He had no idea what to do. The baby was beginning to cry, and the fisherman thought that perhaps he was hungry. When he got home, he would give him some fish to eat, he decided.

2

"Give fish to a baby?" exclaimed the fisherman's aunt. "Are you crazy?"

The fisherman did not have a wife, and so he had called for help from his aunt, who was married to the man who ran the village shop. At first she had not believed him when she received the message that there was a baby and her advice was needed. But when she arrived at the fisherman's house, she found the fisherman trying to feed the baby a small piece of fish that he had cooked and put in a bowl.

"He's hungry," said the fisherman.

"That may be so," said the aunt. "But you don't give such a small baby solid foods like that."

"Not even fish?" asked the fisherman.

"Not even fish," said the aunt. "And anyway, where did you get this baby?"

The fisherman told her the story. As he did so, the aunt took the baby and wiped the small bits of fish from his face. "Poor little thing," she said. "You've been abandoned, haven't you?"

"Whoever did it was very cruel," said the fisherman. "He could easily have drowned."

The aunt nodded. "Well, he's safe now, I'm happy to say. And we can take him into town and hand him over to the babies' home. There's a place that takes babies—orphans and the like. They'll look after him." She touched the baby gently on the cheek, comforting him. "Shall we give him a name?"

The fisherman thought for a moment. "Bobby," he said.

"Why Bobby?" asked his aunt.

"Suits him," said the fisherman.

"All right," said the aunt. "Bobby it is. Bobby Box, because he was found in a box."

"Good idea," said the fisherman.

They took Bobby into town in the fisherman's old car. The aunt sat with the baby in the back because the springs in the front were broken and the baby would have a softer ride that way. After half an hour of bumping and bouncing, they found themselves outside a rather grim-looking building on which the words HOME FOR BABIES (AND SMALL CHILDREN) were carved in stone above the front door. And beneath that, there was a bell with a small notice that said, *All orphaned or lost babies welcome. Ring for attention.*

The aunt rang, and after a minute or two the door was opened by a woman wearing a blue dress and a small, starched white cap. She looked down immediately at the baby in the aunt's arms. "Oh no!" she sighed. "Not another one!"

3

So it was that Bobby went to live in a babies' and children's home. And that was where he stayed for the next six years. He was not very happy there—the beds were hard and lumpy and no matter which way you tried to lie, you could never get really comfortable. And that was not the only thing that he did not like about the home: the food was another problem, and the bullying, which nobody did anything about.

The food first. There was never quite enough of it, and there was not a single child, not one, who did not go to bed hungry. Now, waking up hungry is bad enough, but going to bed with hunger pangs gnawing at your stomach is another thing altogether. You lie there, feeling the sides of your empty stomach clinging to your ribs, and think about food. You cannot help it—no matter how hard you try. You just think about food. You think about large pieces of bread, thickly spread with butter and red jam. You think about cakes, and chocolate, and pies covered with sweet yellow custard. You think about bacon sandwiches and marzipan animals. You think about apples and plums, and fried potatoes with crispy brown skins. You think about everything you know you will never get.

Then the bullying. Although many of the children who lived in this home were very small, there were some older ones too. These children were ten or twelve or even fourteen or fifteen. They had been there for a long time, and they lived in two rooms at the top of the building. One of these rooms was labeled BOYS and the other GIRLS. The smaller children were not allowed up there and so they did not see that the older children had taken the best beds and the best rugs and the best of everything.

The leader of the older boys was a very fat boy called Ern. He was fourteen and had spiky red hair. He had a bed at the end of the room and it was piled high with the blankets he had stolen from all the smaller children. It could get rather cold at night, but Ern never felt the chilly air once he was tucked up in his bed with its numerous blankets. Down below, in their bleak, cold rooms, the children whose blankets had been stolen had to make do with a thin coverlet, or a doubled-up sheet, and would shiver their way through the night, drifting in and out of sleep, dreaming, no doubt, of icebergs and polar bears.

Ern was a bully. He would grab the smaller children's ears or noses and twist them until their eyes watered. Some of the children's noses were an odd shape as a result of this treatment, and Ern laughed at this. "What's wrong with your nose?" he would crow. "Walked into a door?"

Did Mavis Broon, the woman who ran the home, know that this was going on? She did. Did she do anything to stop it? She did not, not even when she saw Ern helping himself to the younger children's food.

"Don't eat too much, Ern," she said mildly.

"No, I won't, don't worry, Mavis old girl," said Ern, popping into his mouth potatoes meant for the smaller children, who would go hungry as a result.

That was the way it was, and that was what Bobby had to put up with until shortly after his sixth birthday, when Mavis Broon sold him to a farmer who wanted a boy to help him to look after his sheep and help cut the hay. She was not meant to sell the children, but she did, spending the money on whisky, which she drank at night, in her room, listening to the radio playing dance tunes until well past midnight.

4

There was more to eat at the farmer's house. So that was one thing that was better in poor Bobby Box's life, even if there was little improvement in other respects. His bed was just as uncomfortable, and his room, which was reached by climbing up a small wooden staircase in the barn, was just as cold. It was lonely—sleeping out in the barn with only the animals for company—and scary too, as when he was woken up one night by a great owl that had flown into the barn and was swooping around, trying to find a way out.

But the real problem was the work, which went on from the crack of dawn until the last rays of sunlight faded from the sky. It seemed to Bobby as if the farmer never did anything but work; he was always up first, walking around the farmyard, feeding the hens or fiddling with this or that bit of farm equipment. Then, during the day, he would be walking through his fields or driving his tractor while Bobby chased after stray sheep or did some other task set for him by the farmer. And this was how it was every single day, with no time for rest.

"We don't need to bother with school," said the farmer. "Waste of time, school."

Bobby did not reply. The farmer tended to become moody if you disagreed with him on anything, and so Bobby just bit his tongue. He wished that he could go to school like other children. He wished that he had parents, as other children had. He wished for so much, but it seemed that he never got anything that he wished for, and so he tried to stop wishing. If you don't wish for anything, he thought, then you won't feel so disappointed when you don't get it.

He spent four years on that farm—four long, hard years. Four harvests, cutting hay with a scythe until his back and arms ached. Four winters, carrying hay up to the sheep, taking load after load until his hair was covered with hayseeds and his nose blocked with tiny pieces of dried grass. Four springs and four summers of weeding vegetable beds and breaking the hard earth with fork and spade.

Then, just after his tenth birthday, he decided to run away. I'm not a slave, he thought. I don't have to work here all my life for nothing.

He would have liked to write a note to the farmer to tell him that he was going, but he could not write. Nobody had bothered to teach Bobby to read or write, and now he could not even leave a message to say good-bye. He did know, however, how to write the letter *B*. And so he wrote that on a piece of paper and left that on the kitchen table along with a small present of a couple of feathers he had found on the hill, a flower he had picked from the roadside, and a green stone he had found at the edge of the river and had polished until it glowed with hidden light. The feathers meant: *I have gone, I have flown away*. The flower meant: *I do not think badly of you*. And the stone meant: *I shall not give up. I shall not be broken*.

He left in the early morning one day, before even the farmer had got out of bed. Packing his few possessions in a small bag, he walked down the farm track and onto the road that led off in the distance to the places he had heard of but could only just imagine—the cities of Scotland where the great ships were made and where the sky was filled with the smoke of factory chimneys.

He was filled with a sense of freedom. There was nobody around now to tell him what to do. The sky above his head was his and his alone; the air he breathed was free. And nobody, he thought as he lifted his head in the morning air, could take the sun away from him and switch it off.

After walking for four miles, he stopped to rest at a place where the road ran beside a small stream—what in Scotland we call a *burn*. He took off his shoes and socks and put his feet in the deliciously cool water, relishing the feeling of water between his toes. He closed his eyes and listened to a bird calling high in the sky above him. Then he opened his eyes and saw that a large truck had stopped on the road behind him.

The driver got out of his cab and came down to where Bobby was sitting beside the burn.

"What are you doing?" asked the man.

"Sitting here," said Bobby. "I'm walking to Glasgow." Glasgow was the name of the place he was heading for; he was not sure where it was, or how far away, but that was where he was going.

"Hop in," said the man, nodding in the direction of his cab. "Come on."

Nobody had ever told Bobby that one should never do a thing like that, and so he did not waste any time. Pausing only to put his socks and shoes back on, he climbed up into the cab and they set off.

"Don't bother going to Glasgow," said the man. "I can give you a job."

Bobby did not want to work on a farm again and started to tell the man that before he was cut short.

"I'm not a farmer," said the man. "I run a circus."

Bobby had never heard of circuses and asked the man to tell him what they were.

"Circuses are big shows," said the man. "They take place in a big tent and move from town to town. There are clowns and trapeze artists and performing dogs. There are two fierce lions and a lion tamer. There are dancing horses and a ringmaster who wears a red coat and a top hat." He paused, looking quizzically at Bobby. "Interested?" And then, without waiting for Bobby to answer, he said, "Good. Well that's settled then."

S

The circus was camped on the edge of a small town, on a piece of waste ground. Well before they reached it, the man, who was called Mr. Macgregor, had pointed out the tent in the distance, with its large red notice saying *Macgregor's Circus.*

"That's us," said Mr. Macgregor. "And you see those caravans over there? That's where you'll stay with the other children."

"Other children?" asked Bobby. "Who are they?"

"Acrobats," said Mr. Macgregor. "Funny bunch. Nobody knows where they come from. Nobody speaks their language, you see. But they're very good at their job, you see, and that's the important thing. Their act brings the house down every night."

There was a question that Bobby wanted to ask, and now, as they approached the circus ground, he asked it. "And my job, sir? What will I be?"

Mr. Macgregor took one hand off the steering wheel and stroked his chin thoughtfully. "Lion tamer's apprentice," he said at last. "Old Jimmy Macdonald is getting a bit slow and has been talking about retiring. Yes, that'll be the best place for you to be. It's a good job, and if you learn young, you learn quickly. That's what I've always said."

Bobby swallowed. He had never seen a lion, but he had heard a bit about them. And what did he know about lions?

Not much, he decided. Except that they had great manes around their heads and . . . and they ate people. He swallowed hard again.

6

Mr. Macgregor took him straight to his caravan and showed him in. It was not a large caravan, but somehow they had managed to fit eight bunks inside. At the far end was a pile of suitcases, out of which socks and shirts and other items of clothing spilled.

"You keep your things over there," said Mr. Macgregor. "And that's your bunk. Happy? Good. It's getting a bit late now, so I think you should go to bed so that you'll be ready to start learning tomorrow."

He smiled at Bobby and gave him an apple. "Have this for your dinner," he said. "Lion taming is hard work, and you'll need to get a bit stronger."

Bobby was not sure what to do. He wanted to tell Mr. Macgregor that he really was not all that keen on lion taming, but he did not know how to say it. So he took the apple and ate it before he slipped into his bunk bed and closed his eyes. The journey had tired him and he was not long in getting to sleep, missing entirely the return of the acrobats an hour or two later. So he did not see the seven other children come in, leaping and bouncing, somersaulting into their beds.

7

"So you're the new boy," said Jimmy Macdonald. "What do you know about lions, may I ask? Nothing? Just as I thought.

Still, I suppose we all have to learn somewhere. We aren't born with a knowledge of lions, are we? Hah!"

They were standing in front of a large cage on wheels. In the cage, lying down on a pile of straw, were two of the largest creatures Bobby had ever seen. These were the lion and lioness, Leo and Leona. They had their eyes closed, although Bobby thought that Leo had one eyelid slightly open and was watching him.

"The thing about lions," said Mr. Macdonald, fiddling with the catch on the door to the cage, "is that you have to let them know who's boss. If a lion thinks you're afraid, then you're in trouble. The moment he senses that, well . . ." Bobby waited for him to finish the sentence, but he did not.

"I've lost so many assistants in my day," Mr. Macdonald went on. "Let me think of them." He held up a hand and counted the names off against his fingers. "Tommy, Micky, Boris, and George."

There were four names, and Bobby suddenly noticed that there were only four fingers on Mr. Macdonald's hand.

"Looking at my fingers?" said the lion tamer. "Yes, that's right—only four of them."

"What happened?" asked Bobby in a small voice.

Mr. Macdonald pointed at Leo. "He got it," he said. "Nasty creature."

Bobby stared at Leo, who seemed to open one of his eyes a little more to return the stare.

"So," said Mr. Macdonald. "No time like the present to get started. You go in there now and give them their breakfast. This bowl of meat here. Put it on the floor in front of them, but whatever you do, don't turn your back on them. Understand?"

Bobby took the bowl in trembling hands. "Do I have to?" he asked.

"Yes," said Mr. Macdonald. "You do. What's the use of being a lion tamer's apprentice if you won't give them their breakfast? Be reasonable, young man!"

On legs that felt like jelly Bobby made his way into the cage. His hands were shaking and his heart was beating within his chest like a great steam hammer.

"Don't look frightened!" murmured Mr. Macdonald from behind him. "Remember—you're the boss!"

Bobby laid the bowl down. Leo had opened both eyes now and Leona was stirring from her sleep. He took a step backward and . . . tripped.

The next thing he knew he was on his back, looking up at the roof of the cage. There was a growl from Leo, and this encouraged Bobby back onto his feet. Getting back up, he noticed that Leo was standing directly in front of him and had opened his mouth to roar.

"Tell him to sit!" cried Mr. Macdonald.

"Sit!" Bobby shouted. "Sit, Leo!"

For a moment the lion seemed confused, but then he suddenly sat down. Without turning his back on him, Bobby inched his way back to the door of the cage and slipped out to safety.

"Well done," said Mr. Macdonald, patting him on the back. "You're a natural lion tamer, young man! I'd say that you've got a good chance of making it, you know. At least fifty percent chance, perhaps even a bit more. We'll see."

8

A few days later, when the circus was ready to perform, Bobby was called into the caravan occupied by the costume maker. Measuring him up, she fitted him with a circus outfit of red coat and striped black trousers. This, she explained, is what lion tamers traditionally wore. The jacket, she said, was one that had been used by the last apprentice. "I've sewn up the holes that the lion's teeth made," she said. "They make a terrible mess, those lions. Horrible. Big gashes in the material—it's an awful waste of good cloth."

Resplendent in his new uniform, Bobby watched as the other circus performers practiced their tricks. The children from the caravan were very impressive: they wore sparkling silver outfits that were caught in the spotlights and sent dancing diamonds of light about the sides of the tent. They tumbled and cartwheeled, swung from bars, made towering human pyramids, all the while calling out to one another in the language that nobody understood.

Then there were the horses. Sporting headdresses of feathery plumes, they cantered round the ring, women in sequined costumes riding on their backs and waving to empty seats that would soon fill with crowds.

And then there was a performing dog, Rufus, who walked on his hind legs round the ring, leapt through a ring of fire, and, at the end of his act, sat down at a miniature piano and played "Camptown Races" with his paws.

Bobby watched all this openmouthed; he was thrilled by

what he saw, but inside he felt cold with fear. Sooner or later, the bars of the lions' cage would be erected around the circus ring and he would have to go in with Mr. Macdonald, holding his whip for him and helping him to position the stools upon which the lions would be made to balance. He did not see why lions should have to do this. What sense did it make to force a great wild creature to do silly tricks for the amusement of humans? What sense did it make to force a boy of ten to help with all this?

9

The people arrived for the performance. From his place near the entrance to the tent, Bobby watched as the seats filled up. Everyone was chattering with excitement, the children enjoying the candy floss and sugar-covered apples bought for them by their parents. Bobby watched enviously. Nobody had ever bought him a sugar-covered apple; nobody had ever bought him anything.

He wondered what it would be like to have parents. He wondered what it would be like to sit next to your parents at a show like this, secure in the knowledge that at the end of the show you would be going back to your own home, to your own room, and not to a caravan shared with seven acrobats in shiny outfits.

He looked across the tent to where a boy of about his age sat between his mother and his father. The boy's father was pointing something out to his son, and the boy was listening attentively. Then they both laughed—they were sharing a joke. If only I could change myself into the boy, thought Bobby. If only I could be him rather than me.

The band began to play. This was the signal for the beginning of the circus, and the grand parade came in to start the show. There were the shiny acrobats; there were the prancing horses; there was the performing dog; there was the wall-of-death rider with his roaring motorbike; there were the trapeze artists with their rippling muscles and strong arms.

Bobby watched as the performers walked round the ring, bowing to the applause of the crowd. Then he noticed a man and a woman sitting at the end of one of the rows of seats not far away. They were staring at him, he thought. He looked away, but when he looked again, he could see that their eyes were still fixed on him. Then the man got up and came over to his side.

"You look very unhappy," the man said. "Is there anything wrong?"

Bobby nodded. "Yes," he whispered. "There is."

10

The man and the woman crept out of the tent, accompanied by Bobby.

Standing outside in the darkness, they asked him his name.

"I'm called Bobby Box," he said.

"And where are your parents?" asked the man. "Where's your mother or your father?"

Bobby looked down at the ground. "I don't have a mother or a father," he said.

The woman touched him gently on the shoulder. "What are you doing here?" she asked. "Do you work in the circus?"

Bobby explained to her about being the apprentice lion tamer. As he spoke, she glanced at the man, and they both drew in their breath.

"Is this true?" asked the man when Bobby came to the end of his story.

"All of it," said Bobby.

"Then you must come with us," said the man. "You don't have to be a lion tamer if you don't want to be! Nobody can force anybody to be a lion tamer, can they, my dear?"

His wife nodded her agreement. "It's quite out of the question," she said. "You must come and live with us. We'll take good care of you."

Bobby hesitated. "And can I go to school?" he asked.

"Yes," said the man. "Of course you can. There's a good school very near our house. You can go there next week, once the paperwork is done."

They walked away from the tent. As he left the circus behind him, Bobby felt a great weight of anxiety lift off his shoulders. And when he heard the lions roaring in the distance as they were prepared for their act, he was not even the slightest bit frightened. He was now an ex–apprentice lion tamer, and there was no reason for an ex–apprentice lion tamer to be afraid of lions he would never see again.

11

The man and the woman were the kindest people Bobby had ever met. In fact, he had not known that there were kind people in the world; now he did. They took Bobby back to their house, which was a large one with a garden that ran down to a river. They gave him a large dinner, one that ended with chocolate ice cream. Bobby had never tasted ice cream. He had never tasted chocolate.

Then he was put to bed in a room that they explained would be his from now on. "We have never had children," said the woman. "Now you have come to us and you can be our son. Would you like that?"

"Very much," said Bobby.

The next day they took Bobby into town and bought him new clothes. Then they went to an office where some papers had been prepared to make it possible for him to be their son. That all went smoothly. A man in a dark suit asked Bobby whether this was what he wanted.

"Of course it is," said Bobby. "Thank you very much."

"And will you be a good son to them?" asked the man in the suit.

"Yes," said Bobby. "I promise I will."

"Good boy," said the man in the suit. "Then that's all legal. Well done!"

12

Bobby was very happy. He went to school now, and they discovered there that he was remarkably good at mathematics, poetry, art, history, chemistry, and football. He soon found many new friends and was given ten parties all in a row, day after day, to make up for all the birthday parties he had missed in his earlier, unhappier life.

The man and the woman were happy too. "We always wished for a son," said the man. "And now we have you. We are very lucky."

"And I'm lucky too," said Bobby. "Really lucky."

13

You may think this a strange story, but it is not. There are people whose lives are every bit as unusual as Bobby Box's—I can promise you that. Not all of them end as well, of course. For many people, the world is a place of sadness and sorrow, which is a great pity, as we have only one chance at life, and it is very bad luck if things do not go well.

But even if you think they are not going well, you can still wish, as Bobby Box did. And sometimes those wishes will come true, as his did, and the world will seem filled with light and happiness. That can happen, you know. So never give up hope; never think that things are so bad that they can never get better. They can get better, and they do. And if you have the chance to make things easier for another person, never miss it. Stretch out your hand to help them, to cheer them up, to wipe away their tears. Stretch out your hand as that man and that woman did to Bobby Box. Stretch out your hand and see what happens.

JEANNE DuPRAU

PEARL'S FATEFUL WISH

Pearl's friends, if you could call them that, were Candy, Bitsy, Farah, Arabella, and Ronette. On the April Saturday when Pearl made what she would later call her Fateful Wish, they had all been at The Stores. It was chilly out, so the vast underground mall was the place to be. All afternoon, they careened down the wide corridors, pressing up against the windows, swarming inside the shops they liked and clustering around the glass displays, arguing about which purse or ring or poster was best, with their voices high-pitched and their hair bouncing and their shopping bags swinging against each other's legs. Pearl wanted a fuzzy scarf to keep her neck from getting cold, and once she found one—a too-bright chartreuse, which Bitsy said was totally gorgeous—she would have gone home if she hadn't been with everyone else.

Around four they got on the Y train and rode back home to Asphalt Area Building #31. Two of the eight elevators were out of order, so Pearl and her friends and twelve other people milled around in the lobby for almost twenty minutes, waiting for one that wasn't too crowded to fit into. The lobby door didn't close right anymore, so wind came in and blew around the grit and paper scraps on the floor. Pearl kept an eye on the scraps in case any of them might be, for instance, torn-up love letters or messages from terrorists, but as usual they were mostly burger wrappers and pizza ads.

The girls (they were all thirteen) giggled and bumped their hips around and gave each other little punches and slaps, and (except for Pearl) they jabbered without stopping.

"You lie!" shrieked Arabella, and Candy said, "I do *not!*" and laughed and shoved Arabella against the wall.

"Pearl," said Farah, "didn't you just *adore* that pink purse?"

"Yeah," said Pearl, trying to remember which purse she was talking about.

"Look, look," cried Bitsy, holding out her hands. "Did you see my new polish? It's called Neon Night."

"I love it!" That was Farah.

"No, yuck! It's too orange!" That was Ronette.

"You're just *rude, rude, rude!*" Bitsy shoved Ronette, and Ronette crashed into a woman carrying three shopping bags, and the woman yelled at her to knock it off, and a man placed his hand under his large, square chin and said he was fed up to *here* with broken elevators and loud kids. Pearl thought, *I am not loud,* but she didn't say anything.

There was a ding, and the up-arrow light above elevator 4 went on. Everyone surged toward the door, which opened and let out at least twenty people. Pearl wormed her way through the outgoing stream. Inside the elevator, she punched the button for Floor 58 and backed into a corner, and all the others squashed themselves in. Candy was in front of Pearl, stepping on her toes, and Farah, who was fatter than usual because of her puffy jacket, pressed against her side. It was hot in the elevator, and Farah's Phantom Gardenia perfume filled the air.

One thousand, three hundred and nine people lived in Asphalt Area Building #31. Most of them, of course, Pearl didn't know, but she knew quite a few by sight because of taking the elevators. Today she noted the tall bald man from Floor 28 with the angel tattoo on his shoulder, the Nigerian family from Floor 14, and the old woman who walked with a walker from Floor 59. There was also Mrs. Pollock, who was the cafeteria lady at school, and Mrs. Norman, who had eight kids, and the quiet woman with round glasses, and the unfriendly woman with the skinny dog, and the fat-bellied man who smelled like onions. All of them were squeezed into the elevator, along with five or six people Pearl had never seen before.

Pearl and her friends knew each other because they all lived on the same floor. If they hadn't, Pearl might not have spent so much time with them, since they didn't have all that much in common. She liked shopping, sometimes. She liked laughing and teasing, sometimes. But the other girls liked these things almost *all* the time. That was the main difference between them and her. She tried not to let it show too much.

Bye, bye, bye, they all said to each other, see you tomorrow, let's go to The Stores again! Let's go get ice cream! Don't forget, Bitsy, I want to borrow Neon Night. Farah, don't tell anyone what I told you! I hate you, Ronette, unless you lend me your shoes, don't forget! They flounced down the doorway-lined halls in different directions, some to the east wing, some to the west, and Pearl went right and then left and then right again to apartment 5819.

Her brothers, Ray and Cam, didn't look up as she came in. Robot cartoons were on TV. The baby, Tessy, banged an empty plastic pop bottle on the floor. From the kitchen came the sound of a spoon clinking against a pan and the voice of the radio news. Pearl went in and sat at the kitchen table.

"There you are," said her mother without turning around. "Would you do something for me? Take this can opener back to Fran? I borrowed it from her. Ours broke."

"Okay," said Pearl. "In a minute, all right? Can I have a glass of orange juice?"

"Be my guest," said her mother.

Pearl got her juice and drank it slowly, listening to the radio. The announcer said that on this day, somewhere in the world, the nine billionth human being had most likely been born. "We've reached that remarkable figure sooner than expected," the announcer said. "Forecasters predicted we'd get there by 2050, and here we are with six years still to go."

Pearl tried to fit the concept of nine billion people into her mind. In the Asphalt Area, there were fifty buildings just like #31, and fifty more in the Graveyard Area, and fifty more in the Hardpack Area. And these were just places out on the edge of the city. *In* the city lived thousands and thousands more. Millions more. How many millions were in a billion? Pearl couldn't remember. She had the feeling that often came over her, as if a swarm of flies were buzzing around in her head.

Whenever this happened, she knew it was time to get away

to someplace quiet, where she could replace the buzzing with interesting thoughts. She liked to invent stories about the lives of the people in the building. The man with the angel tattoo, for instance, might actually *be* an angel in disguise who flew at night from one building to another, solving troubles and granting wishes. The unfriendly woman with the skinny dog could be hiding twelve refugees from Transylvania in her apartment. Pearl also liked to ponder large questions, like "What happens after you're dead?" and "What would it be like if gravity suddenly let go?" She couldn't think this way when she was around her friends or her family. She had to be in a quiet place. The problem was finding one.

"Trans-city report," said the kitchen radio. "H train currently stalled between 383rd and ZZ Avenue. Expect forty-minute delays."

"Back off!" shouted a cartoon robot on the TV. "Zap, zap, out of my way!"

Pearl washed out her glass, standing at the sink next to her mother, who was pouring soup from cans into a pot. "Here you go," her mother said, handing over the can opener. "Dinner in ten minutes, or as soon as your father gets home."

Fran lived in 5804 and was Candy's mother. When Pearl rang the bell, Candy answered the door. "This is your mom's," said Pearl, holding out the can opener. She heard Candy's two sisters arguing about something in loud voices.

"Want to meet up after dinner?" Candy said. "We could go down to Basement 5." In Basement 5 of #31 were two Ping-Pong tables, eight video game machines, and some concrete ramps where you could skate.

"No," Pearl said. "I have homework." This was true and not true. She did have homework, but she was planning to do it some other time.

"Don't be so *boring!*" Candy said.

"I can't help it," said Pearl.

There was a lot of commotion at dinner because Ray made a fuss about eating his broccoli and Cam went on and on in a loud voice telling the plot of yesterday's *Tank Wars* episode, and the baby spilled her grape juice, which dripped over the edge of the table onto the rug, so Pearl's mother had to get a wet rag right away and clean it up. In the background, the radio explained recent hurricane patterns.

Pearl ate fast and set down her fork. Her mother was still in the kitchen, washing out the rag. "Candy wants me to go down to the basement with her," Pearl said to her father, which was not a lie.

"Fine," said her father. "Have fun."

On her way out the door, making sure no one noticed, Pearl grabbed her jacket and her new scarf from the bench where she'd left them. She went down the hallway, turning left, then right, then left again, passing 5820, 5821, 5822, and all the other apartments where people she knew and people she didn't know were eating their dinners, watching their TV shows, having arguments, laughing at jokes, or discussing the state of the world, and when she got to the elevator, she pressed the up button. After five or six minutes, the elevator arrived, the doors opened, and she went in, not noticing that Candy, Ronette, and Arabella were just coming around the corner from the east wing.

They noticed her, though. "Hey, look!" Candy said, pointing at Pearl as she stepped into the elevator and its doors closed. "She *is* coming down to the basement after all. She told me she had homework."

"But look, the elevator's going up," said Arabella, pointing to the lit arrow above.

"Why would she go up? Nothing's up there but the roof."

"The roof is so *boring*," said Candy.

From the south wing, Bitsy and Farah showed up. "Pearl's gone to the roof," said Candy.

"Maybe not," said Arabella. "Maybe she's gone to see someone on Floor 59 or Floor 60."

"Maybe there's a cute boy up there and she doesn't want us to know about him," said Ronette.

"Selfish!" cried Bitsy.

"I hate her!" cried Farah.

"Let's go up! Let's find her! Come on!" Candy poked the up button, and they waited, practicing dance steps and cheerleading moves, while the elevator went up and then came down again.

Pearl by then was on the top floor of the building, which was 61 but had no official number. It was the floor where the air-conditioning units were, and rooms for big vacuum cleaners and carpet steamers and repair tools. At the end of a hall was the door to the stairs. A sign on it said NO ENTRY, but it wasn't locked. Pearl opened it and went in. She flipped the light switch, and a dim fluorescent glow lit up the small room, which always gave her the beginning of a peaceful feeling. To her right stood some green trash bins as big as football players; to her left rose the stairs, which she climbed. At the top of the stairs was an-

other door. This one simply said ROOF. Pearl opened the door
and looped her new scarf over the inside doorknob and then
over the outside doorknob, so it wrapped around the edge of
the door and kept it from closing. It was the kind of door that
locked from the inside, which in Pearl's opinion was dumb—as
if burglars might climb up the side of a sixty-story building to
get in.

She stepped onto the roof. It was a huge expanse of graveled
tar paper, uncomfortable to sit on and ugly to look at, with
short sticky-looking pipes poking up from it here and there and
a few white splotches of bird poop. A high railing of vertical
bars stood around the edge to keep people from jumping off the
building and killing themselves. A couple of big rectangular
structures housed some kind of machinery that made hoarse
breathing sounds in the summer. There was nothing at all to do
on the roof. Nobody ever went there, and that was why Pearl
liked it.

She walked to the edge and looked out through the railing at
the vast view, past the huge upright rectangles of the buildings
like her own, out to more and more buildings beyond them, and
then to the winding silver wire of the river and the clusters of
tall thin skyscrapers far away in the center of the city. Highways
curved and crossed down there, and though she was too high
up to make out separate cars, she could see motion on the highways, like blood cells inching through clogged arteries.

Above all this was the sky. It was not the same sky you saw
from ground level. That sky was chopped into pieces at the
edges and looked small and far away and somehow sad. The sky
you saw up here made you remember the hugeness of the Earth

and the even greater hugeness of the universe. This sky was the only place big enough for Pearl's mind to stretch out in, the only place quiet and empty enough to give her imagination room to work. If she didn't come here now and then, her brain filled up with that swarm of buzzing flies. She realized that she was odd in this way. No one else she knew felt the same, and that meant that even though she was surrounded by people all the time, she often felt lonely.

Right now, the edges of the sky were a smudgy gray-pink, and the tremendous sky-bowl overhead was dark blue, like a deep, deep lake upside down (or so Pearl imagined, though she had never seen a lake). A few stars shone. Pearl gazed at them, trying to imagine the distance between the stars and the Earth, which was even more impossible than trying to picture nine billion people. She wondered if planets circled any of those stars, and whether people might have to go to another planet when this planet couldn't hold them anymore.

She took a long breath of cool air. Then the roof door burst open, and Candy shrieked, "She *is* here! I knew it!" and at once voices were all around her. You went *up*! We saw! Why are you *up* here? It's so boring! It's cold! Farah thought you found a cute boy on 59! Ha, are you kidding, there're no cute boys in *this whole building*!

Arabella grabbed the sleeve of Pearl's jacket and tugged. "You know Amy from Floor 59? We saw her in the elevator. She just got that new movie! We're going to her place to see it!"

"It's called *Crystal Kisses*!"

"Lymon Barry is in it!"

"And Rissa Peele!"

"Come on, come on, we can do our toenails while we watch!"

"Hurry up!"

"What's wrong with you?"

"Come *on*!"

Pearl felt fury boiling up in her like lava from a volcano, and though she tried for a second or two to stop it, she could not. Out of her mouth came a blast of truth.

"I don't *want* to!" she cried. "I do—not—*want* to!" She raised her voice, and the fateful words flew out: *"I wish you would all just leave me alone!"*

The girls shut their mouths. There was a moment of silence. They'd never heard Pearl talk this way. They were stunned.

Candy was the first to recover. "Okay!" she said. "We hate you too!" She whirled around and headed for the door, and the rest of them followed.

Ronette looked back over her shoulder. "Have fun! Don't come looking for us!"

Bitsy was the last one out the door. "Love your scarf," she said, sweeping it off the doorknob where it was hanging. She slung it around her neck.

"Wait!" yelled Pearl, but Bitsy just flipped the end of the scarf, and the door closed behind her.

And locked.

Pearl ran to the door and pounded on it, but no one came.

For a moment, she stood still, facing the locked door, her hands balled into fists. Her heart was drumming. She took a few breaths and stepped back. She told herself it didn't matter that she was marooned on the roof. She wanted to be here, after all.

She had *said* she wanted to be left alone, though maybe she hadn't said it in the nicest way. Anyhow, someone would come and get her eventually. Her father would remember that she'd said she was going to the basement with Candy, and he'd go and look for her and Candy would tell him—but wait. He wouldn't find Candy because she wouldn't be in the basement, she'd be at Amy's. Oh, well. One of her friends would come and open the door, sooner or later. If they were still her friends, now that she'd screamed at them to leave her alone. She probably shouldn't have yelled. Being marooned was her punishment for yelling, probably. She felt like one of those people in fairy tales whose wishes came true in terrible ways.

But she was stuck here at least for a while, there was no way around it. So she decided she might as well enjoy her stuckness, and at first she did. She took in the view from all four sides of the building, and as the sun sank, she watched the orange glow in the west fade to a dusty peach. Somewhere out there, far, far away, were the city limits. She imagined a road called The City Limits Highway that went all around the entire city, with buildings and pavement on one side and fields of grass and yellow flowers on the other. She could see it exactly in her mind. There would be benches next to the fields where people like her could sit and think. Or read. Or make up songs. There would be birds that weren't pigeons or crows.

After a few minutes, the sun went behind the horizon and became no more than a rusty smudge of light far away, and Pearl's neck, with no scarf around it, began to get cold. When the sun disappeared completely and a small, sharp wind came up, all the rest of her got cold too. The roof became a field of darkness. Her imagination, usually her friend, turned its other side and began showing her the bad things that could happen: she could freeze; she could trip over a chimney pipe and break her leg; she could stumble and fall against the railing, and the railing could collapse, sending her sixty stories straight down.

She would have to find a way to get off the roof, because she knew that soon she would start to be afraid.

In apartment 5819, Pearl's mother brought out chocolate pudding for dessert. "Where's Pearl?" she asked.

"She went down to the basement with her friends," Pearl's father said.

"Oh, all right," said her mother. "Here, Tessy, have some pudding, and try not to get any in your hair."

In apartment 5922, six girls sat on the rug eating microwave popcorn and watching *Crystal Kisses*, enthralled by the sapphire eyes of Lymon Barry, who had put his hand on Rissa Peele's shoulder and was drawing her toward him. Through Candy's mind flitted one stray thought about how weird it was that Pearl would rather stand around on the roof than see this movie. Pearl was a really strange person, she thought, and after that she didn't think about Pearl again, nor did any of the others.

Pearl decided to try stomping and yelling. She knew that the roof she stood on was not directly over anyone's apartment—it was over that top floor that had no number, with the maintenance rooms and air ducts and plumbing and trash bins. But it seemed possible that a loud enough noise might go all the way through that floor and penetrate down into the next one, and someone might hear her.

So she stomped as hard as she could, back and forth across the roof, shouting, "Help, help, help!" Then she galloped for a while, making horse noises, and then she jumped with both feet, as if squashing a long row of bugs: thud, thud, thud, thud.

No one came.

The old woman who walked with a walker heard a distant pounding and called the building supervisor to complain about something wrong with the heating pipes. She got the usual recorded voice: "Supervisor's hours are from nine to five Monday through Friday. Please leave your message after the tone."

Dinner was over in apartment 5819, and the dishes had been washed.

"Didn't Pearl say she had homework tonight?" asked Pearl's mother.

"I don't know," said her father.

"She's been down in the basement quite a while," said her mother. "She shouldn't spend so much time hanging out with those friends of hers."

"I'll go find her," said Pearl's father. "Which basement is she in, do you think?" Asphalt Area Building #31 had eighteen basements.

"Usually she goes to 5," said her mother.

Pearl's father went out the door and along the halls to the elevators, where he punched the down button. After seven and a half minutes, the elevator came and he got in.

Eight minutes later, he arrived in Basement 5 and discovered no girls there, only an elderly man asleep on the couch and two boys playing pool. "Did you see a girl here, about your age, short brown hair, wearing a green T-shirt?" The boys shook their heads and went back to their game, and Pearl's father punched the button for the elevator again, trying to remember the apartment number of the girl named Candy.

Making noise got Pearl nowhere. She had to think of something else. She put her back to the locked door and leaned against it, shivering. Out in front of her loomed the boxlike structure that held the noisy machinery. Maybe she could find a way off the roof through there. She might be able to get inside and wriggle through an air duct. She'd seen it done in bank-robber movies—men slithering along through pipes, sort of like going down a slide headfirst.

She walked out into the darkness slowly, so she wouldn't trip, and felt her way around the walls of the machine shed until she found a low door. The door wasn't locked. She opened it, stooped over, and took one careful step inside, into a clammy-cold, pitch-black space that smelled of oil. There was another smell, too, that she faintly recognized. What was it? She stood still, sniffing. Beside her left foot something moved— a rustle, a skittering. With a shriek, Pearl leapt backward. Rat droppings, that was the smell. She slammed shut the door and staggered away. Horrible, horrible! Rats on the roof, and they would come out at night! She shuddered; she felt sick.

She got herself to the edge of the building again and held on to the railing with one hand. Think, she told herself. Calm down and think. She was about to freeze into a girl-shaped ice cube. She had to get someone's attention. Could she drop something over the side of the building and hope a person going by below would notice? If she had a piece of paper and a pencil, she could write a note: "Help! I'm marooned on the roof of Asphalt Area Building #31!" She could put it in one of her socks, weight it down with her lip gloss and a few coins from her pocket, and throw it over the railing, hoping it didn't land on some ledge or flagpole and never make it to the street. But even if it *did* make it to the street, who would notice a balled-up sock? They'd think someone threw it out the window. People threw stuff out windows all the time.

Anyway, she didn't have any paper, and she didn't have a pencil.

Pearl's father couldn't remember the number of Candy's apartment, so he had to go home again and ask his wife, who told him it was 5804. He went there and rang the doorbell. Candy's sister Mindy answered—she was getting ready to go out and had purple eyeshadow on one eye but not the other—and said that Pearl wasn't there and neither was Candy and she didn't know where they were.

"Maybe your mom knows," said Pearl's father.

"Mom, where's Candy?" Mindy yelled.

"Down in Basement 5," the mom yelled back.

"No," said Pearl's father. "I looked. She isn't there."

"She's not there," Mindy yelled to her mom.

"Well, then she's in one of the other basements," the mom called. "She's always down there somewhere."

Mindy smiled and shrugged. She shut the door and went back to her mirror.

Pearl's father was stumped. Maybe Candy was always down in the basements, but Pearl wasn't. He began to worry a little.

Pearl saw a flurry of motion out there in the dark. Ack! Was it rats? She picked up her feet and danced backward a few steps, then stood still, peering and listening. The wind riffled her hair. Nothing else moved. Something brushed against her leg, and she jumped wildly sideways—but when she reached down to swat it away, her hand came up with a nothing but a feather.

She steered her mind away from rats and focused on the only thing she could think of that might save her. There were people on Floor 60. They were closer to her than anyone. She had to make one of them know she was here.

She calculated. The utility floor just below her was maybe ten feet high. Floor 60 would begin below that. Every apartment had four tall windows. How could she get to one of those windows and knock on it? She would have to climb up the railing and down its other side. She'd have to hold on to one of the metal railing bars with her left hand, hang there above the thousand-foot drop, and somehow thump on a window ten feet below. To do this, she would need a ten-foot rope with something heavy, like a rock, on the end.

She didn't have a ten-foot rope, and she didn't have a rock, and she knew she didn't have the nerve to climb the railing and hang off the side of the building. Thinking about it made a cold sweat break out on her hands. But the picture in her imagination helped. It just needed some adjustments.

The bars of the railing were about four inches apart. A small dog or cat could get between them, but not a person. Pearl put her face close to the bars and looked down—not all the way down to the tiny streetlights, just a little way down to the windowsills of Floor 60. Below her she saw three of them, narrow concrete ledges, visible because light was shining on them from inside the windows. And light from the windows meant someone was inside. Right down there was the person who could save her.

She wished she had an arm ten feet long. Then it would be easy: she'd just slip her hand between the rods of the railing, drop down her long, long arm and knock on the glass of the window. She didn't have such an arm, of course, but as she imagined this, she saw how she might make one.

She sat down. The gravel poked painfully at the seat of her pants. She unlaced the boot on her right foot, took the boot off, and pulled the shoelace out of the holes. It was about two feet long. She did the same with the other boot. When she tied the laces together, she had a string almost four feet long, which was not nearly long enough. She took her socks off. They were knee socks, each one more than a foot long when stretched out. When she added the socks to the shoelaces, her rope was, she guessed, almost seven feet long. Still not long enough.

She took off her jacket. The wind sliced into her, but she steeled herself against it. With an effort, she tied one sleeve of the jacket and one end of a sock together. From the end of one sleeve to the end of the other, her jacket was about four feet long. Her rope now looked like this: jacket, sock, sock, shoe-lace, shoelace. She thought it might be long enough. She threaded the last shoelace through one eye of one boot and made as strong a knot as she could.

Finished. Also barefoot, with numb toes.

She pushed the boot between the bars of the railing, making sure she was right above one of the lighted windows, and care-fully, carefully, she began to lower her rope. With her forehead pressed against the bars, she watched until the boot hung just above where she thought the window ought to begin. It wasn't quite far enough down. It would thump on the side of the building, not on the glass, and the person inside wouldn't hear it. She needed another six inches or so, that was all.

And she had it. Though her arm wasn't unnaturally long, it was long enough. She put it between the bars and stretched it downward until her shoulder was against the railing and the cold metal pressed against the side of her face. Then she flung her arm outward and felt the boot at the other end of her rope swing a little way out from the building and fall back toward it.

Bang.

She heard the sound, boot heel against glass.

She made it happen again, over and over. Bang. Bang. Bang.

At last there came a scraping, sliding noise, and a voice, sounding annoyed. "What's *out* there?"

Pearl yelled with all her might. "HELP!" she cried. "I'm on the roof! I can't get down! It's Pearl, I can't get down, please help me!"

• • •

Pearl's father came into the kitchen, where Ray and Cam were eating ice cream out of a carton and the baby was banging a spoon against the table leg. "I can't find Pearl," he said. "Do you know where she went?"

They said no.

He went into the bedroom, where Pearl's mother was asleep with a folded washcloth over her eyes. He decided not to wake her up, not yet; she was having one of her bad headaches. He decided to go down to the basements again. He'd try every one of them.

In apartment 5922, the movie was almost over. Lymon Barry had kissed Rissa Peele, and they were now strolling hand in hand along a beautiful wide avenue beside the ocean, with the sun setting in glorious color beyond them.

"So beautiful," said Arabella.

"I wish it was me," said Ronette.

They watched and sighed as Lymon and Rissa clasped each other in a long embrace that was silhouetted against the blazing evening sky.

"Pearl's going to be sorry she missed *that*," said Candy.

"Should we go tell her how good it was?" Bitsy wondered.

"Or do we still hate her for yelling at us?" said Farah.

They decided they didn't hate her anymore, and after the movie credits had finished rolling, they trooped down to apartment 5819 and arrived there as Pearl's father was coming out the door.

"Aha!" he cried when he saw them. "But where's Pearl? I thought she was with you."

"No," said Candy. "She wanted us to *leave her alone.*" She rolled her eyes. "Isn't she home?"

"No," said her father.

They all stood looking at each other.

Down the hall and around two corners, the elevator door opened, and out stepped Pearl and a middle-aged woman wearing round glasses, a gray sweatshirt, and a baggy blue corduroy skirt. Pearl had a thick pale blue blanket wrapped around her. When she and the woman got to her hallway, Pearl started to run. "Dad!" she yelled. The blanket flapped.

Everyone stared at her.

"I got stuck on the roof!" she said, coming to a stop in front of them.

"Stuck?" said Candy.

"The door locks from the inside," said Pearl. "You locked me out."

"We did not," said Arabella, but she looked uncertain.

"We wouldn't do that!" said Ronette.

"We didn't *know*," said Bitsy.

Pearl gave Bitsy a withering look. "I want my scarf back," she said.

The woman with the glasses spoke up then, addressing Pearl's father. "I'm Margaret Golub," she said. "Apartment 6033. Your interesting daughter caught my attention."

Pearl had saved herself in more ways than one, as it turned out. Margaret Golub was a writer who spent most of her days sitting at her computer, trying to finish the novel she had been working on for seven years. When something had thumped her window and she'd opened it and heard a voice calling, she had rushed up to the roof and brought Pearl down to her apartment. She'd wrapped her in a blanket, given her hot apple cider to drink, and waited until she had warmed up enough to stop shivering. Pearl had explained to her how she happened to be marooned on the roof, and because Margaret seemed the sort of person who would understand, she also explained that she was on the roof in the first place because sometimes she needed to have enormous spaciousness and silence around her, to give her room for her thoughts and imagination, and it was hard to find anyplace that wasn't crowded and noisy.

"You could come here," said Margaret. "It's always quiet here. Sometimes I talk to my cat, but otherwise—utter silence."

After that, Margaret's apartment became Pearl's Special Silent Place. She went there often.

Margaret worked in a corner room, at a desk with a computer on it and nothing else. "I can't have clutter around," she told Pearl. "Clutter makes my mind fog up." Margaret's mind, it turned out, was rather like Pearl's. Pearl had buzzing instead of fog, but they both needed space and quiet to clear their minds out and think the thoughts they needed to think. It made Pearl happy to have met another person like herself.

In Margaret's living room, beside the very window that Pearl had knocked on, was a wide green armchair. "When you're here," Margaret said, "this can be your chair."

Margaret laid out the rules. Pearl could knock on Margaret's door any weekend morning between 8:30 and 9:30. She could stay for as long as two hours, and there would be no talking until after 11:00, when there might be some if they were both in the mood. It was good to have the rules clear. That made it easy for Pearl to go to Margaret's without feeling shy or as if she was intruding. She got into the habit of going once a week, and sometimes twice. She would gaze out at the view from Floor 60, stroke the cat, and think her thoughts. Sometimes she brought a book with her and read. Sometimes, after 11:00, she and Margaret talked a little, and now and then they had lemon cookies or leftover Chinese food.

Pearl apologized for yelling at her friends. She explained to them that sometimes she had to be by herself, and it wasn't their fault. After that, they didn't tease her as much for being strange, and she enjoyed herself more when she was with them.

Bitsy had come over the day after the roof incident with Pearl's scarf draped around her neck. She took the scarf off and handed it back to Pearl. "I wouldn't have taken it if I'd known the door would lock," she said. "Really, I wouldn't."

"That's okay," said Pearl. She thought how remarkable it was that her Fateful Wish—to be left alone—had come true twice, first in a bad way and then in a good way. If it hadn't been for Bitsy, neither the bad part nor the good part would have happened.

She felt a little surge of gratitude toward Bitsy. It wasn't Bitsy's fault that she was different from Pearl in a few ways, like having a different kind of mind and different taste in colors. "You can keep the scarf," she said. "It looks better on you."

JANE YOLEN

WISHES

There is a moment in every wish,
a trembling, a small slippage,
a fracture along a seam of the mountain
where consequence and desire meet.
You do the after-you no-after-you step,
the one where you meet someone
in the street, the school hall, the locker room
and spend awful moments trying to decide
who goes left, who goes right, who goes through.
We want so much,
we want so much not to want.
Wanting makes us weak, weakly we accept.
I will take what is given, give what is taken,
only do this for me first.
The wish spoken.
The deed done.
The mermaid trades her tail for legs.

The miller's daughter gives her unborn up for gold.
Jack takes the goose, the harp, and hacks down the stalk.
All for what?
The tail was better than the legs.
The girl should have stayed at the mill.
Jack became the villain, not the hero.
We should be giving wishes away,
not taking them.
The old tales have it wrong.
Those kind of wishes gift us
a moment of fulfillment,
a lifetime of regret.

MEG CABOT

THE PROTECTIONIST

Every man has his breaking point. For me it was when I found the piece of paper taped to my little sister's back that said, *Boobies: Get some*.

"Dave," Jenny said when she saw my expression. She'd had no idea. Who knows how long she'd been walking around with it stuck back there? "I don't care. I don't even want boobs. They'll only get in the way of my front walkover roundoff back handspring, which everyone says is so good, it's sure to land me a first at the Kirkland Ranch tumbling invitational tonight."

Jenny may not have cared, but I sure did.

"He's gone too far this time," I said as I scanned the cafeteria. Cody Caputo was never too hard to find. He was the biggest kid in our class, the only kid at Highland Estates Middle School able to eat an entire pepperoni-and-sausage pizza for lunch every day. "When you use offensive graffiti to verbally harass a victim because of her gender, it's called a bias crime."

"Dave," Jenny said, looking nervous. "Can't you just forget it?"

"Forget it?" I echoed. "Are you serious? Would you have asked that question of John Maynard Keynes, the father of modern macroeconomics? Or professional BMX bike racer Aaron Weinstein? What if they'd just *forgotten* it? Where would we be today?"

"Oh, geez," Jenny said, rolling her eyes. "Here we go."

That's when I heard Cody's big dumb laugh floating toward us from nearby the "You Can Achieve Anything If You Try!" posters that hung over the trash bins. He and Rick Cardoza and Austin McFeeley were pointing in my direction.

"Look," Cody shouted, his mouth full of cheese and processed meat. "I never noticed until today, but Shrimp Newburg's sister's got even less of a rack than he does!"

This was uttered at a decibel level so loud, everyone in the entire cafeteria had to have heard it.

I didn't even glance at Jenny. I think she reached out to try to stop me—she usually does—but it was too late. Who cares if Cody Caputo is the biggest kid in our class and I'm the smallest? John Maynard Keynes missed a great deal of school as a young man in the late nineteenth century due to poor health, but did that stop him from saving the British economy during World War I by amassing scarce currencies, such as pesetas, then selling them off at just the right time, in order to break the market? It did not.

Of course, Cody Caputo was not alive during World War I and so did not stuff John Maynard Keynes headfirst into a trash bin for his efforts.

"Looks like someone didn't want to finish their *Shrimp Newburg,*" Cody cackled with his friends as they fled the scene of the crime. At least I think that's what he said. It was hard to hear with all the chunks of leftover meat pizza in my ears.

"I don't know who wouldn't want to finish such creamy, delicious Shrimp Newburg," Rick Cardoza said, cracking himself up.

I wasn't able to extract myself from the trash bin until they were gone. Not because I'm the slightest bit afraid of them, of course, but because the bin was so slippery inside, what with all the ice cream sandwich wrappers.

When I finally emerged, Jenny was there, holding some paper towels for me.

"I told you it was better just to forget it," she said. Fortunately, by that time, all of her friends from the gymnastics team were gone as well.

"I can't just forget it," I said. "Cody's gone too far now that he's brought you into it. He's a complete sociopath, you know." When Jenny looked a little blank—I sometimes wonder how we can even be related, let alone have spent nine months side by side in the same womb—I explained, "Someone lacking in a sense of moral responsibility or social conscience. When bullies like him are allowed to flourish in our society, they tend ultimately to be elected to public office or made into celebrities on cable news shows. I can't allow that to happen with Cody."

"You have sausage in your hair," Jenny said, handing me more paper towels.

"They won't get away with this, Jen," I assured her. "It's one thing to call me Shrimp Newburg—which doesn't even make sense, since I'm well within the national height range for our age group. But no one makes fun of your lack of development and gets away with it."

Jen sighed. "Please don't say you're going to go tell Vice-Principal Bushey about this. I'm not going to be able to rescue you if they retaliate by taping you up in the boys' toilets again after school, because I'll be at the Kirkland Ranch tumbling invitational."

"Don't worry," I said. I held up the sign I'd pulled off her back, which I'd kept from getting stained by sealing it in the clear plastic sheath I wear every day in the right front pocket of my shirt. While this is derisively referred to by some as a "pocket protector," it really does come in handy for protecting things, such as forensic evidence. "I have proof this time."

Jenny just shook her head. "It's your funeral," she said.

It was while waiting for my meeting with Dr. Bushey that I saw *him* for the first time. At first I thought he was at Highland Estates for a job interview, maybe as the new custodian.

Except that most grown men don't bring their mom to a job interview.

"Highland Estates is a Blue Ribbon Honors School, Mrs. Garcia," Dr. Bushey was saying to the lady who was standing next to the kid. She was only half her kid's size but looked exactly like him, minus the tiny mustache he had growing on his upper lip. "Only the best schools in the country achieve that kind of recognition from the U.S. Department of Education."

"Thank you, Dr. Bushey," Mrs. Garcia said gratefully. "I'm sure Amado will be much happier here than he was at his last school."

Amado Garcia? That was the name of this kid, who was so large he made Cody Caputo look like one of Jenny's Polly Pocket dolls? Poor guy. *Amado mio* means "my beloved" in Spanish, a fact I happen to know because I am in all AP classes, including Accelerated Languages.

Amado didn't look as if he much appreciated his mother naming him the Spanish equivalent of *my beloved,* much less moving him to a Blue Ribbon Honors School like Highland Estates. He was scowling . . . at his mom, at Dr. Bushey, at Dr. Bushey's administrative assistant, Miss Rivera, who is really very attractive for someone of her advanced years, and finally at me.

It was like being scowled at by a walking bulldozer.

Except that this bulldozer was wearing an official Aaron Weinstein Yeti Shok Jok BMX racing shirt. Just like the one I had back in my closet at home.

Only Amado's had to be size triple XL, which makes it highly unlikely his mom, like mine, bought it in the children's department at JCPenney.

"And I certainly hope you'll try out for our basketball team, Amado," Dr. Bushey said. "I understand you were quite the star on your old school's team. First in your division? And Coach Caputo is considered one of the best middle school coaches in the state."

I couldn't help making a slight gagging noise. It wasn't my fault. It was a reflex. Coach Caputo is Cody's dad.

"Oh, Dave." Dr. Bushey noticed me for the first time. I could sense his disapproval at my having shown up in his office wearing a shirt covered all over in pizza sauce in front of a student who might prove to be such a valuable addition to the Highland Estates Panthers. "I wasn't aware that we had an appointment today."

"We don't," I assured him with a wink. "But no need to worry. There hasn't been a repeat performance of what happened last week. Yet."

The fact that people have started to call me Ginger Dave— and have started to write that name all over my locker door in permanent marker—as well as Shrimp Newburg is also thanks to Cody Caputo. Though I suppose it's nice of him to try to mix it up. If it weren't for people calling me names, no one around school would call me anything at all, as I'm almost universally ignored.

"Great," Dr. Bushey said, sending a nervous glance in the direction of Mrs. Garcia. "Great to know. Why don't you come in, then? I always have time for my students!"

"It's true," I assured Amado and his mom as I made my way into Dr. Bushey's office. "Dr. Bushey has an open-door policy. Especially for students with special needs."

I tried to give Amado a meaningful look as I said the words *special needs,* to let him know I was *simpático.* After all, Amado and I both had crazy names (it's unbelievable how many different types of seafood you can smother in Newburg sauce) and seemed to have gotten shafted in the growth hormone department as well.

But apparently Amado didn't understand my look—or maybe he just didn't consider himself someone with special needs. He barely glanced at me at all, as a matter of fact, except to avoid me like I was some kind of freak, just like everybody else.

I don't know what I was expecting. Why would someone as cool as Amado obviously was ever want to be friends with someone like me? Next week, he'd probably be dumping me in the garbage along with the rest of Coach Caputo's basketball team.

Following my presentation to Dr. Bushey of the forensic evidence of Cody Caputo's sexual harassment of my sister—I'd spent fifth period dusting the *Boobies: Get some* paper for prints using some of my mom's old eye shadow and a roll of clear packing tape I always keep in my backpack for emergencies, and found that the prints (as well as the handwriting) matched those taken from my locker door last week; I then matched *those* prints to some I'd taken from a Coke can Cody threw at my head—I was told by Dr. Bushey that he would call Cody into the office to "discuss the situation with him."

I should have known that this wasn't going to be the end of the matter, however. The last two times Dr. Bushey had called Cody into the office to "discuss the situation with him," I'd wound up taped to a urinal by Cody and his cronies.

The fact is, getting division trophies is all Dr. Bushey thinks about. He'd never do anything to make Coach Caputo mad— such as tell him that his son is a complete sociopath—or risk his winning streak or make Coach Caputo consider moving to another school district.

But those other times, I hadn't had definitive *proof* that it was Cody who'd written *Ginger Dave* all over my locker or threw things at my head (it was his word against mine). This time, I did. Surely Dr. Bushey would have to expel—or at least suspend—someone who was going around putting *Boobies: Get some* signs on girls' backs, no matter how great a coach his dad was . . . especially in light of actual forensic evidence of his participation in the crime.

Except that I guess forensic evidence doesn't matter if your dad has won as many district tournaments as Cody's has. That's the only explanation I can think of for why, when I arrived at the rack where I lock my bike every morning, I found my official Yeti Shok Jok BMX racing bike—identical to the one Aaron Weinstein will be using in next month's UCI World Championships in Val di Sole, Italy—missing.

Cody was thoughtful enough to leave a note, and in his own handwriting. If this isn't flagrant disregard for the law, I don't know what is:

This is wat hapens to snitches, ginger. Call the cops, and YOU'll be nex.

This note did not even make grammatical sense. Did Cody mean that if I called the police, he was going to cut *me* in half with a pair of bolt cutters, the way he had the chain I'd used to lock my bike?

Or that he was going to steal me, the way he had my bike?

It was hard to know for sure.

Every great man has had to overcome hardship during the course of his lifetime. John Maynard Keynes suffered attacks from both the left and right for his economic models, considered by some to be too progressive, and yet by others to be too conservative.

And after shattering his spine in a snowboarding accident at the age of twelve, Aaron Weinstein was told he might never walk—much less engage in recreational sports—ever again.

But neither of these men ever had to deal with an obstacle like Cody Caputo, an extremely poor speller who was nevertheless well above average when it came to the art of torture, especially of persons smaller than himself.

I am not John Maynard Keynes. I am not Aaron Weinstein.

And in my own defense, Cody and Rick and Austin live in the same subdivision that I do. I didn't want to run into one of them before I'd had a chance to formulate some kind of plan. They couldn't *all* have ridden my bike home. At least two of them had to be taking the bus—the same bus I took. If I got on the bus, they'd be there, waiting for me. I'd be outnumbered.

Surely John Maynard and Aaron would have understood this, if they'd known about it.

So I decided to walk home—three whole miles. Dad, I knew, was still at work in the city, and Mom was driving Jenny to the Kirkland Ranch tumbling invitational. I doubted either of them would have been particularly sympathetic if I'd called to ask for a ride, anyway. They'd both warned me when I bought my bike (with the money I earned helping all the residents in Grandpa Newburg's assisted living community set up Skype accounts so they could chat live with their grandkids) that I'd be the only kid in my whole school with an official Yeti Shok Jok BMX dirt tracker—the most expensive dirt bike on the market—and thus would probably draw the envy of my peers.

This information had actually only made me even *more* eager to purchase one.

Now I wished I had listened to them.

By the time I got home, the sun had almost set. A single star shone down above the golf course just behind our backyard.

As I drank thirstily from the bottle of Sunny D Mom had left in the fridge—why hadn't our city planners thought to place a single convenience mart between Highland Estates Middle School and the gated subdivision in which my parents so unwisely chose to make our home?—I gazed upon the star and thought about the song Grandma Newburg used to make Jenny and me sing back when we were little and Mom always dressed us alike.

Later, when everyone was home and gathered around the dinner table for Chinese takeout, I asked, "Do you guys believe that whole thing about when you wish upon a star, your dreams will come true?"

"Of course, sweetie," Mom said. "Pass the mu shu pork."

"What's your wish, bud?" Dad asked.

"That I had a friend," I said.

Mom dropped the mu shu container.

"I'm your friend, bud," Dad said after he'd managed to get down the Mandarin chicken on which he'd been choking a little. "So's your mom. And Jenny."

"You're family," I said. "You don't count. I mean a *real* friend, my own age, who could help me with . . . well, stuff."

"Wishing on stars doesn't work," Jenny said. "If it did, I'd have a pony by now, considering how often I've wished for one. And don't tell me that video game you guys bought me counts. I'm twelve, not four."

"You have lots of friends, Dave," Mom said, shoveling mu shu back into the container. "Who was that boy I heard you talking to the other night?"

"That was Rajit," Jenny said. She twirled the gold medal she'd won at her invitational at the ends of her fingers. "He lives in India. He and Dave were playing *Aaron Weinstein: Extreme BMX Dirt Trax* online. Dave only has virtual friends because Cody Caputo's made everyone at school so— *Ow.*"

She glared at me because I'd kicked her under the table.

"Cody Caputo?" Mom echoed. "You mean Coach Caputo's son? What about him?"

"Nothing," I said quickly. "He's just a bit of a *boobie.* Don't you think, Jen?"

She turned bright red.

"Yeah," she said. "Never mind."

"What were you trying to do back there?" Jenny hissed at me later, as we loaded the dirty dishes into the dishwasher after dinner. "You think I want to discuss my boobs in front of Dad?"

"You think I want to discuss getting stuffed in a trash can in front of Mom?" I demanded.

"Well, what are you going to do about it?" she asked. "You can't go around saying you wished you had friends to help you and not expect me to explain to Mom and Dad what you need help *with.* And you *could* have friends, you know, if you worked harder at it."

"What are you talking about?"

"Do you think wishes just *happen*?" she demanded. "Stars are busy. They can't sit around all day, making every single one of our wishes come true all by themselves. They need a little help from us. I know if I really want a pony, I need to be like you and go out and earn the money to buy one, like you did with your bike. But I've been busy working on my other wish—having the best front walkover roundoff back handspring in the state. Which, by the way, I do." She dangled her medal in front of me.

I blinked. I had never thought of wishes this way. Jenny didn't know it, of course, but she'd basically just summed up the neoclassical microeconomic model.

"How am I supposed to work at making friends?" I asked her. "I thought friends just . . . happened." They certainly seemed to for Jenny. She had billions.

"Well," she said, "for one thing, it might help if you didn't go around talking about that old dead guy and Aaron Weinstein so much."

Old dead guy? Did she mean . . . she couldn't. *John Maynard Keynes?* He was certainly more than some old dead guy. And Aaron Weinstein? Aaron Weinstein was known, in BMX circles, as the Golden Child, a fact of which Jenny was obviously not aware.

I decided to forgive her, however, considering she was being so informative.

"And if people didn't think that by associating with you they'd get taped to a urinal by Cody Caputo, well, that might help, too," she went on. "What happened with Dr. Bushey, anyway?"

I didn't want to tell her about my bike. No one had noticed it was missing from its usual place in the garage.

"He's going to speak with Cody," I said stiffly. "Everything's going to be fine."

"Oh, I'm sure," Jenny said sarcastically. "Just like last time. Look, Dave. People would probably like you a lot if they knew you as well as I did. Treat making friends the way you did getting that bike you wanted. Make it like a job, not a wish. Okay?"

I don't know what I ever did to deserve a sister like Jenny. But I'm pretty lucky, I guess.

Later that night, Dad tapped on my door.

"Hey, bud," he said. "Just checking in. Anything you might, I don't know, want to talk about?"

I lowered my copy of *The General Theory of Employment, Interest, and Money*, to which I often turn in times of distress.

"Yeah, Dad," I said. "There is. Do you think you could give me a ride to school tomorrow? The Shok Jok's got a flat."

Dad winced. "Oh, sorry, bud," he said. "No can do. Gonna be gone before you get up. Early meeting. But I'll leave you money on the counter so you can get that flat fixed. How's that? Have a good night, now."

Sometimes parents are great, even when they're blundering around without the slightest idea what they're doing. Aaron Weinstein's mom, for instance, bought him his first dirt bike at a garage sale after the doctor said he'd never snowboard again, just because she thought biking might be therapeutic for him, since he couldn't walk so well with his broken spine and all.

If it weren't for Mrs. Weinstein, Yeti Shok Jok, now a multi-million-dollar corporation, might never have been born.

I don't know if either of John Maynard Keynes's parents

ever did anything quite that supportive, but mine have certainly had their moments.

I wouldn't say the next morning was one of them, however.

"I'll see you after school!" Mom said, blowing me a kiss as she drove off to her Pilates class, for which she was late, and which was in the opposite direction of the school.

So she couldn't give me a lift, she said, when I tried to give her the same story I'd told Dad about my flat.

"Your bike doesn't have a flat tire," Jenny said as we trudged to the bus stop together. Mom and Dad might have fallen for the flat-tire excuse. But I'd never been very good at pulling anything over on Jenny for very long. Maybe because we'd spent so much time swimming around in Mom's uterus together. "Your bike's not even in the garage. What happened to it?"

That's when Cody Caputo, whose timing could not have been more awful, happened to ride by on my Yeti Shok Jok. It looked good, still shiny black, with no major dents. At least he hadn't been abusing it.

"Hey there, ginger *saps*," Cody called as he whizzed past.

Jenny sucked in her breath.

"Dave," she said, her eyes narrowing. "You told me that everything was going to be fine. But everything is *not* fine, is it?"

She did not stop haranguing me on this subject until the bus trundled up.

I wasn't worried, though. Because Cody wasn't on the bus. He was on my bike. This meant I didn't have to worry about whatever Cody was going to do to me next for at least a half hour.

I'd forgotten that while Cody might not be on the bus, his cohorts would be. That's how Jenny got her first-place gymnastics medal stripped from around her neck first thing by Austin McFeeley, who tossed it to Rick Cardoza.

Rick shrieked, "Ew, I can't believe you touched it! Now you've got gingivitis!"

"You guys." Jenny's face was very red. "Give it back. Now."

"Yeah, you guys," I said. I could tell my face was red, too. And not just because people were saying I had gingivitis. I didn't have any friends on the bus who would let me sit by them. I'm a bit of a lone wolf, which is why I like bike riding so much.

By lone wolf, I mean I don't have any friends. Except, as Jenny pointed out, Rajit, who lives in Mumbai.

The bus driver didn't improve matters much by yelling, "You! With the red hair! *Sit down!*"

Only I couldn't sit down, because every person with an empty space on the seat next to them kept saying "This place is saved" and putting their backpack there whenever I came near.

"Keep it away from Shrimp Newburg!" Austin screamed.

Jenny's medal went flying over both her head and mine.

It was like a nightmare. I was starting to wonder if I'd even woken up yet. Maybe I was still in bed. I especially wondered this when a large number of people on the bus started chanting, "*Shrimp* Newburg, *Lobster* Newburg, *Crab* Newburg."

I really ought to have just claimed a fever and stayed home.

Then suddenly, from out of nowhere, a huge fist shot up into the air. It closed around Jenny's award, then came down.

"Here," Amado Garcia said, holding Jenny's medal out toward her.

She looked down at his palm, which was about the size of a soccer ball.

"Th-thanks," she said, and nervously plucked up her medal, then dropped it back around her neck and darted to the seat some of her friends from the gymnastics team had saved for her.

"Redheaded kid!" the bus driver yelled, giving me the evil eye in his rearview mirror. *"Sit down!"*

The nightmare wasn't over—but it had definitely taken a turn for the better. Austin and Rick had sunk down into their seats and were staring at Amado in astonishment. Amado, in turn, was looking at me like I was a piece of gum stuck to the bottom of his shoe. There was no one sitting by him, of course, because he was so gargantuan—and new—everyone was already afraid of him. Even more afraid of him than they were of Cody Caputo's gang.

And that, of course, gave me an idea.

Inspiration often appears from out of nowhere, kind of like stars over the golf course. What made Mrs. Weinstein buy that rickety old dirt bike for Aaron? What made John Maynard Keynes buy up all those pesetas?

Who knows? The fortunate thing for all of us is that they did.

"Is this seat taken?" I summoned all my courage to ask Amado Garcia.

He sighed, looked up at the ceiling of the bus, then scooted over a fraction of an inch to make room for me on his seat.

"The name's Newburg," I said, flinging myself on the seat beside him. "David Newburg."

"Really," Amado said. "I did not get that your last name was Newburg."

Then he lowered his sunglasses and sank down in his seat, pretending to be asleep.

But I persisted.

Because, like Jenny said, when you have a wish, you have to work to make it come true.

"Why'd you help my sister like that?" I asked.

Amado straightened and lifted his sunglasses, his gaze flying toward Jenny. All you could really see of her was her copper-colored ponytail bobbing up and down above the back of her seat as she chattered excitedly with her friends.

"That's your *sister*?" he asked, in tones of astonishment.

People always say this. But if you asked me, Jenny and I look a lot alike. Except for the ponytail, of course.

"We're fraternal twins," I explained. "Identical twins are always the same sex. And you didn't answer my question. Why'd you help her?"

"I don't know," Amado said, lowering his sunglasses again with a sigh. "I guess I don't like it when guys pick on defenseless girls."

Defenseless! Jenny? Now I knew something else about Amado, besides the fact that he was an Aaron Weinstein fan and that his mother had named him *my beloved*:

He was nuts.

"Jenny placed first in the Kirkland Ranch tumbling invitational last night with her front walkover roundoff back handspring," I informed him. "That's the most competitive event on the middle school gymnastics circuit. Jenny could probably cut off the circulation to someone's carotid artery using her thighs if she wanted to."

Instead of this information making him less interested in Jenny, as one might expect, it only caused Amado to sit up straight again and stare harder at her through his sunglasses.

"Really?" he asked.

"Yeah," I said. This kid was certifiable. Oh, well. You have to work with what you have. "It's just too bad about those guys back there—and Cody Caputo—making her life such a misery."

"Caputo?" His heavy dark brows knit. "Isn't that the basketball coach's name?"

"Yeah," I said. This was a troubling development. Amado seemed already to have been sucked in by the Highland Estates Panthers. "You thinking of going out for the team?"

Amado shrugged and sank back down again. "Like I have a choice," he said. "Look at me. Coach Caputo showed up at my house last night with two pizzas. He was practically begging my mom to let me play."

I felt my dream crumbling all around me.

"Oh," I said. "So . . . I guess you're on the team now."

"I don't like to commit to things until I've checked them out for myself first," Amado said. "So I'm going to wait till I've been to a few practices to see what it's like."

This cheered me up a little.

"Well," I said. "That's good to know. Because Coach Caputo's kid—"

Amado held up one of his giant hands. "No," he said. "Didn't you hear me? I said I like to check things out for myself. I'm not interested in gossip. I don't play that game."

I considered this. I sure wouldn't want some new kid listening to gossip about me. Ginger Dave. Shrimp Newburg. The kid who always ends up taped to the urinal.

On the other hand, everything I had to say about Cody Caputo was one hundred percent true. I had proof.

"Fine," I said. "But the coach's kid is the bully who's been bothering me and Jen at school. Yesterday he put a sign on her back—I won't even tell you what it said, it was so offensive. That's what I was in the office for when I met you yesterday."

"I thought you were in the office because someone dumped you in the garbage," Amado said, lowering his hand. "That's what it looked—and smelled—like to me, anyway."

"Yeah," I said. "Well, that was Cody, too. After I tried to cannonball him in the gut for what he did to Jen. Then he stole my official Yeti Shok Jok BMX racer—"

"Wait a minute." Amado stared down at me. "*You* have an official Yeti Shok Jok BMX racing bike. An *Aaron Weinstein* Yeti Shok Jok BMX racing bike?"

"Yeah," I said. I knew I didn't look like the type to have a Yeti Shok Jok . . . a scrawny, redheaded, freckle-faced kid like me.

But Aaron Weinstein hadn't looked like the type who could do a 360 when he pulled off his first one, either, considering his body cast.

"But they only made a limited number of those," Amado said.

"Three thousand," I said. "I know. And up until yesterday, when Cody Caputo stole mine, I had one. That's what I wanted to talk to you about. Because I saw you wearing an Aaron Weinstein shirt, and you know one of Aaron's mottos is 'Dudes should always help another dude in need.' I figured if you and I kind of paired up, we'd—"

"What do you mean, paired up?" Amado asked suspiciously.

"I'm a dude in need," I said to him. I hoped I was doing this right. I'd never had a friend before. I didn't know how you asked someone to be yours, really. Jenny had been a little sketchy on the details. "You can see that I'm . . . well, of slightly smaller frame than most of the rest of the kids on this bus. And I have coloring of the reddish variety. There are some people who attend Highland Estates who feel this makes me a freak of some kind. And they torture me about it daily. They're the ones who stole my bike. I want the torture to end. And I want my bike back. I think you can make this happen. Frankly, Amado, I need you. I need . . . well, a protectionist."

"What's a protectionist?" he asked bewilderedly.

"Protectionism," I explained, "is the theory or practice of shielding a country's domestic industries from foreign competition by taxing imports. Most economists argue against it in favor of free trade, as protectionism harms many of the people it's meant to help. But in my case, I can only see it as beneficial."

Amado stared down at me some more. "Are you one of those Asperger's kids?" he asked, not unkindly.

"I don't like labels," I said. "The point is, ever since I got the bike, Cody's had it out for me. I need someone like you in my corner to protect my assets."

"Like a bodyguard," Amado said.

"Exactly," I said. "What do you say? Are you in?"

Amado shook his head slowly. "I don't know," he said.

The bus was rounding the corner to school. I wasn't sure I'd be able to bear whatever taunts would be waiting for me.

Treat making friends the way you did getting that bike you wanted, Jenny had said. *Make it like a job, not a wish.*

Oh, right. I'd almost forgotten.

"Oh," I said. "I'm willing to pay you, of course. Five dollars a day."

He frowned. "That's not exactly what I—"

"Ten," I said.

"It's not the money," Amado said. "It's just that I'm new here. I didn't have any friends where I used to go to school because everyone there judged me by the way I looked. That's why I left. I told you—I don't like gossip because for a while I was the subject of a lot of it, even though it was all lies. I don't want to walk right into the same thing here. Do you know what I mean?"

I stared at him.

"Yeah," I said, my eyes filling up with tears as the bus pulled into the circular driveway right next to the flagpole. "Yeah, I do know what you mean."

It was hard to keep from crying right there on the bus, but somehow I managed not to. I didn't want to cry because I was afraid of what was going to happen to me when I got off the bus. I didn't want to cry because I was so disappointed by Amado turning me down. I wanted to cry because I was so disappointed in *myself*. I couldn't believe that, for a while there, I'd been as bad as Cody: I'd been judging Amado by his looks. I'd thought just because Amado was big, he wouldn't mind being someone's protectionist, their paid thug.

Just like Cody Caputo thought just because I was small, I wouldn't mind being a pushover, someone's punching bag.

Well, the days of being Cody Caputo's victim were over. Just like Amado, I was going to make a new start.

And I was going to do it the way Jenny had said to. Not by wishing it would happen. Not by paying someone to make it happen for me, either, or trying to make people think I was cool because I owned a cool limited-edition bike.

I was going to work at it the way Amado was working at it, by transferring to a new school and starting over. The way John Maynard Keynes defied his critics and saved the U.S. from plunging into another Depression after World War II. The way Aaron Weinstein went from doing bunny hops in his driveway on that rickety old garage-sale dirt bike to doing barrel roll transfers at the Summer X Games extreme sports competition.

Just thinking about these great heroes gave me the courage I needed to step off the bus, walk straight up to Cody Caputo—who was doing some frankly quite pathetic 180s in front of a small crowd of people near the bike rack—and say, "Cody. That's *my* bike. And I want it back now. So hand it over."

My voice was shaking. So were my knees. I jammed my hands into my jacket pockets so he wouldn't be able to see how badly my fingers were trembling.

"Oh, you want it back, do you?" Cody asked, grinning, as he flew past me on my own bike. For a few seconds I thought he was going to ram me with it, and I stepped back instinctively. This caused everyone to laugh. "Well, come on then, Ginger. Come get it."

Everyone laughed some more. There was no way I was going to be able to get my bike out from under Cody Caputo. He was just too big.

"Aw, what's the matter, widdle baby?" Cody asked as he circled by on a second pass. "Is Shwimpy Newburg gonna cwy?"

More laughter erupted.

This was horrible. I was never going to get my bike back.

I needed to face facts: Some men are heroes.

I, David Newburg, am not.

Those posters in the cafeteria, the ones that said "You Can Achieve Anything If You Try!"?

Those posters lied.

Then, as Cody Caputo passed me a third time—faking me out, like he was going to try to ram me—a miracle occurred. Or at least I thought it was a miracle. Something bright and shiny was thrown into his spokes—*my* spokes—jamming the front wheel, and the bike came to such a sudden stop, Cody was thrown over the handlebars into a heap at my feet.

The bright shiny thing was attached to a blue ribbon. The owner of the ribbon pulled on it, and the shiny thing shot from the spokes of my bike and back into the hand of its owner.

My sister.

"Cody," Jenny said, pocketing her gold medal. "Why do you always have to be such a jerk?"

Everyone gathered in the circle around us laughed. Only for once not at me. They were laughing at Cody.

It *was* kind of funny. Cody had such a surprised look on his face.

"I told you," I said to her. "He lacks a conscience. But you don't have to be like this, Cody. People would actually like you—instead of just being so afraid of you that they do whatever you say—if you'd act a little nicer to them."

I stepped over him and picked up my bike. Jenny had bent the spokes a little with her medal, but I wasn't mad. I was pretty sure her medal was bent, too. She'd sacrificed it, and all for me.

Maybe you *could* achieve anything if you tried.

Cody stared at us for a few seconds from the heap into which he'd sunk. Then, with a shriek none of us expected, he exploded.

I'm not sure whom he intended to come after, Jen or me. But he never reached either of us. Because Amado, who'd apparently followed Jenny from the bus, reached out one of his long arms, caught Cody up by the collar of his shirt, and said, "Hey. Didn't anyone ever teach you it's not nice to pick on people who are smaller than you?"

Cody, his feet dangling a few inches off the ground, looked up at Amado and said, "Hey, man, put me down. This isn't cool. We're on the same team."

"Not yet, we aren't," Amado said. "And to tell you the truth, right now I don't know if we ever will be."

Everyone in the crowd said, *"Oooooh."*

"What's going on out here?" A tall man broke through the crowd. It was Coach Caputo. The kids who'd gathered to watch what they'd been hoping would be a fight now scattered, fearing they'd somehow be implicated.

"Dad," Cody cried. "Thank God you're here. Make him put me down!"

"Hi, Coach," Amado said calmly, still holding Cody in mid-air. "I was just explaining to your son here that, based on the fact that I just caught him stealing another kid's bike and trying to beat up a girl, I'm pretty sure I'm not going to be able to join the Panthers. I don't play on teams with people like that."

Coach Caputo did something amazing then. He looked at his son and said, "Cody. Is this true?"

"Of course not," Cody cried. "I was just borrowing that stupid kid's bike. You know him, it's that weirdo Shrimp Newburg, he's the one who's always trying to get me in trouble—"

"Which is why you stole his bike and dumped him in the trash yesterday?" Jenny asked. "And stuck a nasty note to my back?" She turned to Coach Caputo. "My brother gave the vice-principal the note. Dr. Bushey probably didn't show it to you because he didn't want to make you upset."

Coach Caputo looked *very* upset. But not with Jenny or me.

"You can put him down now," he said to Amado. "And you don't have to worry about playing with my son. He's off the team."

"Da-a-ad!" Cody screamed.

To Jenny and me, Coach Caputo said, "I apologize for any difficulties my son might have caused either of you. I can assure you they'll be dealt with appropriately and won't be happening again in the future."

Amado put Cody down. His shirt collar was immediately seized by his father, who started dragging him toward the school and Dr. Bushey's office.

"No, Dad," Cody was crying. "You've got it all wrong. Let me explain!"

But Coach Caputo looked as if he'd heard all the explanations he cared to for one morning.

Amado, Jenny, and I all looked at one another.

"Well," Jenny said, taking her bent gold medal from her pocket and dropping it back around her neck. "I'm glad that's finally settled. Bye."

Then she turned around and walked over to join a big group of girls who'd stopped on their way into school to watch what was happening. As soon as Jenny reached them, they all let out excited little screams, grabbing Jenny's arms and hurrying her into school. They all kept looking back over their shoulders at Amado and grinning.

All except for Jenny. She kept her gaze glued on the school doors as she walked, her ponytail bobbing behind her.

Her face had been very red as she'd said the word *Bye,* though, for some reason.

"You'd better take that bike into the office and ask them to keep it in there for the day since you don't have a lock," Amado advised me, ignoring the girls. "Otherwise someone else will steal it."

I felt overwhelmed. With happiness. With relief. But mostly with gratitude toward him.

"I . . . ," I said. "You . . . That was . . . That was the most amazing thing I've ever seen. I don't know how I can ever repay you."

"It was nothing," Amado said with a shrug. "Like you said, 'Dudes should always help another dude in need.' You don't have to repay me."

"But I do," I said. "History shows that gift economies don't work. We have to have an exchange of goods or services. I don't know what service I can perform for you, and you already said you won't let me pay you—" I looked down at my bike, and it was like a small grenade going off in my head. I knew. I knew exactly how I could repay him. "Here," I said, thrusting it toward him. "Take the bike!"

Amado stared at me in astonishment. "What?"

"The Yeti Shok Jok," I said. "Take it. You deserve it for what you did. You can get those spokes fixed. You'll never know—I mean, really—you'll never know how grateful I am for what you did. Aaron Weinstein would want you to have it. And so do I."

Amado sighed. Considering the enormity of my sacrifice— which I utterly and completely meant, from the bottom of my soul, because friends do these kinds of things for one another, I'm told—he didn't seem very grateful.

"I don't want your bike, Dave," he said. "I have my own Yeti Shok Jok at home. I saved up for months mowing lawns last summer so I could afford it." When I looked shocked, he nodded. "Yeah. I'm just not stupid enough to ride mine to school, because I wouldn't want some idiot like Cody Caputo to steal it."

"Oh," I said, feeling dumb.

Amado shook his head. "Wow," he said. "You really do need a protectionist. You know that?"

As Amado and I walked toward the administrative office, with me rolling the bike between us, I reanalyzed what Jenny had said last night about friends and how getting them wasn't something you could wish for, it was something you had to work at, like having a job. Maybe she hadn't meant a job like an actual labor economy exchange of goods and services. Maybe she'd meant something else.

I tried to remember the conversation I'd frequently overheard Jen having with her girlfriends.

"So," I said, "do you want to get together this weekend?

Maybe we could . . . ride bikes? There's this park by my house that has some really sweet jumps."

Amado shrugged. "Okay. If I don't have basketball practice."

"And maybe afterward," I said, "you can come over to my house and we can play *Aaron Weinstein: Extreme BMX Dirt Trax* online. I have the latest version."

"Will your sister be there?" Amado asked.

"Jenny? Yeah, I guess so," I said. "But I don't know why we'd want to play with her. She's terrible. Mostly during the weekend she just hangs around and practices her jumps in the backyard."

"I'll be there," Amado said.

"Sometimes she makes cookies, but she usually burns them," I warned him, because I thought it was only fair he knew what he was getting himself into. "Then the smoke detectors go off. And sometimes if she gets to the console first, she wants to play this really stupid game where you have to get these ponies ready for this horse show—"

"Hey, Dave," Amado said. He stopped, pushed up his sunglasses, then gave me a smile. "I said I'll be there, okay?"

I stared at him. It was hard to contain my grin. "Why? Are you . . . are you going to be my protectionist?"

"No," he said. "I'm going to be your friend. Save me a seat in the cafeteria at lunch today, okay?"

Then he turned around and went off to class.

I couldn't believe it. It seemed impossible—like a dream come true. But it wasn't. It wasn't a dream.

I had a friend. A real friend.

I wondered if Amado had read *The General Theory of Employment, Interest, and Money.* If not, I would be more than happy to lend him my copy.

Twelve-year-old refugee Beina cooks for her family.
Women and children wait for water.   Photo Credit (both): *UNHCR / H. Caux*

SOFIA QUINTERO

THE GREAT WALL

It started last summer with Lexi's crush on Pete, although we didn't know that was his name yet.

Anyway, first clue: Lexi was "feeling like Chinese" practically every day. It took me years to get her to taste pork fried rice, and when she finally did, Lexi just wrinkled her nose and said, "It's a'ight." Now, not only did she love fried rice, she dragged me to Great Wall three, four times a week. I'm surprised I didn't get sick of it!

Second clue: Great Wall is on the corner of Randall Avenue and White Plains Road—three long blocks away from our building. Meanwhile, there are four other Chinese takeout places along the way. But Lexi complained that China Pavilion wasn't as good, Golden Palace charged a quarter more for a pint of rice, Mandarin Wok just opened and she didn't want to take a chance on a new place, and Five Star was on JJ's block.

And that was the biggest clue of all. For the entire school

year, Lexi made me take the long way to and from school just to pass by JJ's building. Lexi's mother is mad strict and forbids her from leaving our stoop, while my mom is cool, giving me permission to go to the playground and movies. But I'm too scared to go alone, so Lexi sneaks along, but you know what that means, right? It's what the lawyers that work with Lexi's mom call *quid pro quo*. Lexi risked punishment by coming with me to the movies, and I returned the favor by following her while she chased her crush of the month all over Castle Hill.

So I finally figured out that JJ was out and Pete was in when Lexi hounded me to come with her to Great Wall one Wednesday. Mind you, she didn't have enough money for a pint of pork fried rice. "How much you got?" she asked me.

"I'm not blowing it on another pint of pork fried rice for the third time this week," I said. On Mondays before going to work, Mami would leave me ten dollars on the kitchen table that was supposed to last me the whole week. Thanks to Lexi's new obsession, I was down to two bucks and change only halfway through the week. I had already decided to spend my last two dollars on Mr. Softee, but even though he comes every day, I was trying to hold out till Friday.

"Just give me the change, then," Lexi said. "That gives me enough for a pint."

"Fine," I said as I funneled the coins into her palm. "Let's just go to China Pavilion. It's too hot to be walking all the way over to Great Wall." But I shouldn't have forked over the change *before* saying that, because Lexi was already walking in the opposite direction.

Maybe it was the heat that made me realize what Lexi was

up to. I mean, we had been making these runs to Great Wall for
weeks before I noticed that she wasn't acting the way we do
when we go to the pizzeria or the deli. What do you do at any
store? You go in, maybe look at the menu, place your order,
and then go sit down. If there are lots of people and no place
to sit, you wait for your order outside. After walking three
blocks in the nasty humidity, I couldn't wait to sit down once
we got to Great Wall because it isn't just a takeout place with a
giant fan blowing around hot air. It's a small but nice restaurant
with air-conditioning. When we got there, I immediately
dropped into a booth, but instead of joining me after placing
her order, Lexi stayed at the counter, craning her neck and
twisting her curls around her finger. Only then did I realize
that all summer Lexi had been actually *looking* at someone behind the window.

I got up and peered over her shoulder. She was staring at
the delivery boy as he ate his lo mein lunch. No wonder that
first time she wanted Chinese food Lexi suggested we have it
delivered.

"Why?" I said at the time, pointing to the corner. "China
Pavilion is right there." And that's when Lexi first complained
that their pork fried rice was bland. "Well, we're only getting a
pint of rice, and that's only three seventy-five," I said. "The
minimum for delivery is eight dollars, and I'm not blowing all
my money this week on one order."

Lexi finally talked me into going to Great Wall, practically
skipping the entire way, only to be so grumpy on the walk back
to our building. At first I thought she was unhappy with the
food. Now I got it; the delivery boy wasn't there.

I grabbed Lexi by the arm and dragged her outside. "Oh, my God, Lexi, you're, like, all crushed out on the Chinese delivery boy?"

Lexi yanked her arm away from me. "Tell the whole world, Nicole!"

"Sorry!" I didn't think I was that loud, but whatever. I lowered my voice. "Why didn't you just tell me?"

"'Cause . . ." But she didn't finish. Instead, she smiled and said, "He's cute, right?"

I shrugged, and Lexi pouted at me. "What?" It wasn't like I'd been studying him the way she had. I needed to take another look.

Now Lexi's the one grabbing my arm and pulling me back. "Nicole, no!"

"I'm not gonna do nothing." I walked to the fish tank and pretended to be fascinated with them, which is not hard to do. I watched the tetras hover near the surface while the catfish grazed the pebbles at the bottom. There was a single black fish who swam back and forth across the middle of the tank by herself. Soon Lexi was beside me, nudging me to sneak a glance into the kitchen at the delivery boy.

He seemed about sixteen, and his jet-black hair was cut in random layers all around his head with the longest piece dangling over his eye and dyed candy apple red. He also had a metal stud in his earlobe.

"See his tat?" Lexi hissed in my ear. "It's hot, right?" I'd seen the symbol on his wrist before. It looked like the letters *F* and *T* got dressed up and met at a square table. But I couldn't remember what it meant.

"What is it?"

Lexi just shrugged. The girl at the register said something to the boy in Chinese, and he looked up straight at us. She burst out laughing before returning to the kitchen. The boy rolled his eyes at her, muttered something back and continued eating like nothing happened.

Lexi huffed. "She better not be talking about us."

"Oh, she definitely said something about us."

"What she say?"

"I don't know, Lexi! Do I look Chinese to you?"

The girl came back to the register with a brown paper bag, smiling sweetly. "Small pork fried rice," she called out in her thick accent. I hope she didn't think she was fooling anybody. We were the only ones there, so who else's order could it be? I waited outside while Lexi went to the counter and paid. Here I was embarrassed when I wasn't even checking for this guy.

As we walked back to our building, Lexi had what I call a Wonder Moment—when she is full of questions that we can't answer. Every third question or so, she asks me something I *can* answer, but she's on to the next wonder before I can get in a word.

"I wonder what his name is. I wonder what his tattoo means. I wonder why he wears his hair like that. It's kind of cute, right, Nicole? I wonder what that stupid girl said to him. I wonder if that's his sister. You don't think that's, like, his girlfriend or anything like that, do you, Nic? I wonder where he goes to school."

The thing about Lexi's Wonder Moments is that they don't end until she hits a question that we just might be able to an-

swer. Once she has an answerable question, there's no stopping
Lexi, and of course, being her BFF since kindergarten, I get
dragged into her quests for the Answer. Sometimes the quests
are harmless and fun, like when we were eight and tried to stay
up all night on Christmas Eve because Lexi wanted to know
how Santa Claus got the presents into our apartments when our
building didn't have a chimney. Last summer, though, a quest
got us put on punishment for two weeks because Lexi decided
to ask some guys selling drugs on the corner if they were the
ones who hung sneakers on the telephone wires to advertise
their "wares" like she read on the Internet. Somebody told her
mother she was talking to those guys. Probably the lady who
owns the cleaners across the street. She can see everything from
there and has known Lexi's mom since she was our age.

When we got to my apartment and Lexi said, "I wonder
where the Chinese people go after they close their restaurants,"
I knew we were headed for one of those quests that could get
us into trouble, and I didn't want to lose another two weeks of
summer like last year.

"You want lemonade or iced tea?" I said, holding up both
pitchers in front of the refrigerator.

"I mean, haven't you noticed, Nicole?" Lexi reached for the
lemonade and poured it into the glasses she had set on our
kitchen table. "They have all these businesses in Castle Hill—
whole Bronx, really—like takeout joints, that place where we
got our backpacks and those cute barrettes, the nail salons . . ."

I should've kept my mouth shut or changed the subject, but
I couldn't help myself. "I'm not sure, but I don't think those
people are Chinese," I said. "Probably Korean."

In Lexiville, that's the same as saying *So what kind of trouble do you want to get into this week?* There was no turning back to ask her if she wanted to watch TV while we ate, take our plates to the fire escape, or otherwise change the subject. "Still, I don't think any of 'em live around here. Have you seen them? I don't see any of them in school or at the library or nothing."

I thought about it, and she was right. "I guess it's kind of like our moms," I said. "They live here in the Bronx but work in Manhattan. Like a lot of people who live in one place but work in another."

"No, it's different," Lexi said as she scooped pork fried rice onto each of our plates. "My mom works for the City, and your mom works at that college. They're one of thousands of people who work for somebody else. But the Chinese are like the Dominicans that own the bodega on our street. Or the Mexicans on JJ's block. Or the Jamaicans selling *real* beef patties across the street from the pizzeria . . ."

I started to see what she was saying. "Or like the Indian family that owns the video store," I said as I took a bite of rice. All the different people who have businesses in Castle Hill also live here. We weren't just their customers. We were also their neighbors. Then I remembered. "But the video owner's son doesn't go to our school."

"No, but he goes to Blessed Sacrament, which is right there," Lexi said. "And they ain't even Catholic."

"How do you know these things?" Then I remembered. JJ is Indian. In her quest to know anything and everything about him, Lexi must have collected a lot of information about other Indians in our neighborhood.

"The difference, though, is that the Chinese have stores in Castle Hill, but they don't live here like the Dominicans and the Indians and everybody else who have stores here do. It's weird."

I sipped my lemonade and gave it some more thought. "Maybe not. 'Cause if you think about it, as different as they seem, everybody else is from the same part of the world. Even us Jamaicans and the Indians."

"No, the Indians come from the same area as the Chinese," Lexi said.

"Uh-uh. I mean, originally, yeah. Like a million years ago," I said. "But the ones in this neighborhood are specifically from Guyana. That's like a hop, skip and jump from Jamaica."

"No, it's not!" Lexi said. "It's on the complete opposite side of the sea."

"Still." Geography was the one class where Lexi outdid me . . . by a lot. "Guyana's a whole lot closer to Puerto Rico and DR and Jamaica and all those places than it is to India or China."

"True." We stopped to eat for a few minutes. Then Lexi said, "You know what? One night we should wait for Great Wall to close, and then we should follow them home."

It was useless to argue with Lexi, but that doesn't mean I didn't try. Even though I always caved in at the end, I had to put up a fight so if we got caught I could at least tell our moms that I tried to talk her out of it and not be lying.

And the truth was that when I went to bed at night, I kept thinking about the aquarium at the Great Wall. All the different kinds of fish seemed to get along, yet they stuck to their own schools. The tetras stayed together at the top of the tank while the catfish closed ranks near the gravel. Their world in the tank was a lot like my neighborhood. Everyone was friendly when we crossed paths in public, but for the most part, we stuck to our own kind. Not everyone in our neighborhood was like Lexi, who crushed out on guys of all kinds. I wished more people here were like Lexi, especially me. I guess that was why I eventually agreed to her crazy plan.

The plan was to sneak out with our bikes and meet on the corner across the street from the restaurant at midnight. The first time neither of us showed up because we didn't wake up. The next day we each came running to the other with a thousand apologies, thinking that we had stood the other up. After we laughed, we realized we could set our cell phone alarms to get us up without waking our mothers. Then, to be sure, whoever got up first would text the other, and neither of us would go to the corner until we were sure the other was on her way.

The second night, we were wide awake long before our meeting time because a thunderstorm hit and neither of us could sleep. I liked thunderstorms, especially in the summertime, but Lexi was afraid of them, so I worried about her. I texted her first.

QueenNicki: No way we goin out there 2nite
Lexiwithani: Word!

On our third try, we made it to the corner by eleven and stayed crouched behind an SUV until we saw Pete, the girl and their parents exit the restaurant. Lexi was so ecstatic. "See, that's got to be his sister!" she said, punching me in the arm. "Why would she be there so late and leaving with them if she were just a worker or his girlfriend?"

"Ow," I yelled. "Relax, will you?"

"Shhh." Pete and his family climbed into a car, and we jumped on our bikes. "Pray for a lot of red lights, Nic."

"I know, right."

We lucked out to a point. There were a bunch of red lights and stop signs that helped Lexi and me keep up with the car, pedaling like crazy until my legs burned. But then Pete's family's car took a left onto the Cross Bronx Expressway ramp, and it was a wrap for us. No way could we take our bikes onto the expressway. Even if Lexi were *that* crazy, I wasn't.

Still, I had to admit that riding down Castle Hill Avenue at top speed in the middle of the night, with the warm summer air flowing through my cornrows, I felt like a superhero. When I just imagined doing these things, my skin grew cold with fear. But then Lexi got me doing them, and all of a sudden in the middle of it all, I felt like I could fly. I became fearless, and nothing could stop me, let alone hurt me.

For a week Lexi and I didn't try anything because we just had no idea what else we could do. That turned out to be the worst week of our summer. Lexi and I even got into a fight and didn't speak for a few days. All I remember is trying to cheer her up and Lexi not wanting to be cheered up. So I said something I shouldn't have. You know, I threw something in her face that she'd confided in me, using it against her. I can't tell you what it is because I never should have repeated it in the first place, and I still feel bad about it.

The next week I texted Lexi with an apology and a plan to follow Pete.

QueenNicki: Im so sorry. Pls 4give me. I will give u my allowance 4 3 wks. $30!!! We can get a cab to follow Gr8 Wall

Lexi made me wait for a half hour, but she finally responded.

Lexiwithani: I 4give u. Come downstairs so we can plan.

Instead of getting a cab, we bribed this Jamaican girl in our neighborhood named Marcia. People who don't know us sometimes think I'm Marcia's younger sister, which is fine by me. She's sixteen, real pretty and mad cool. Plus, she's got a cute boyfriend who has a nice car that he lets her drive sometimes.

So Marcia got her boyfriend's car that night, and we waited for Great Wall to close. As his father was pulling down and padlocking the gate, Pete and his sister were shoving each other. This was how we found out his name was Pete. Their mother broke them up and scolded them in Chinese when his sister yelled, "Tell Pete to leave me alone, then!" She had no accent whatsoever.

"Oh, my God, they know English," Lexi said. "They speak perfect English."

"Well, duh," I said. "They live here, work here, most likely go to school here. They had to know *some* English." But the truth is I was just as surprised as she was. Unlike Lexi, I was ashamed that I didn't know better.

"Okay, that's not *some* English, Nicole," said Lexi. "She sounds just like anybody on the CW."

Even Marcia laughed as she started the car while Pete's family walked to theirs. But she stopped laughing when they got off the Cross Bronx Expressway and headed to the Whitestone Bridge. "Where are you people taking me?" she cried. "These people are going to Queens!"

"Go, go, go!" Lexi yelled. "Nicole will give you another ten dollars next week." I slapped her in the arm, but what was done was done. Marcia paid the toll and continued to follow Pete's family. And as we crossed the bridge and the beautiful Manhattan skyline cast its reflection onto the river, I was happy that Lexi convinced Marcia to keep driving. Before that night I had only seen the skyline on postcards and TV, and nothing does the real thing justice.

The Great Wall family drove for another fifteen minutes and finally pulled up in front of a brick two-family house just like the ones in our neighborhood. Marcia parked the car a few yards away and turned off the lights and engine. Lexi and I watched from the backseat as Pete, his sister and their parents got out of the car and went into their house.

"Where are we?" I asked Marcia. "In Queens, I mean."

"This is Astoria." Then, before Marcia and I knew it, Lexi had opened the door and dashed across the street. "What is that child doing?"

I ran out after her. "Lexi!" She was in their driveway and almost at their front door. "Are you crazy?"

"Shhh!"

"Don't hush me!" Trying to yell and whisper at the same time hurt my throat. "You're the one trying to run up to Pete's door."

"I am not trying to run to the door," she said. "I just wanted to see the number."

"For what?"

"So that maybe I can send him a card or something."

"You didn't have to run out the car. All we had to do was ask Marcia to back up."

"Well, I didn't think of that," Lexi hissed sarcastically. "Sorry!" That's when we heard her giggling. We were so into our stupid argument in the driveway that we didn't realize Pete's sister was looking down at us from her bedroom window.

I don't know what got into me, but once I was over the shock of being busted, I said, "I want to know what's so funny!"

Lexi finally had a turn at being embarrassed. She grabbed my arm and tried to pull me toward the car, which Marcia had backed up right in front of the house. "Let's get out of here before she calls her parents or something," Lexi pleaded.

"Bad enough y'all think you too good to live in our neighborhood," I said, "but then you front like you don't know much English. That's wack!"

"Hey, it's not like I got a say in where I live. Do you?" Before I could answer, she added, "And you wanna know what's wack? You two chasing after my brother like he's all that. Dude's like a complete tool."

"You're just saying that because he's your brother," said Lexi.

"Doesn't mean it isn't true, though," she said. "'Sides . . . Pete's already got a girlfriend."

Now Marcia was in the driveway. She grabbed both of us and steered us back to the car. "Enough, you two." She looked up at the girl and said, "I'm sorry, we're leaving."

"Whatever." And almost as if she could hear Lexi's heart break from her second-story window, she yelled, "You're way too pretty for him anyway."

Lexi and I climbed into the backseat of the car, and as we waited for Marcia to get to the driver's side, Lexi called out the back window, "And what's your name?"

"Molly," said the Chinese girl. "Like the black fish in our tank at the restaurant."

"I'm Nicole, and this is Alexandra," I said.

"But everyone calls me Lexi." Then she added, "Lexi with an *i*."

We waved to her as Marcia drove away. Lexi didn't ask her to stop at the corner so she could get the name of Pete's street. Nobody said a word, and I don't think any of us was thinking of Pete at all. Molly wasn't anything like we had expected. The way she laughed at and teased us even when she didn't even know our names. The slang she used to express herself whether standing up for herself or dishing on her brother. The way she went from sassing us for following Pete to making Lexi feel better about the fact that he already had a girlfriend. Just because she was Chinese, none of us thought she would be just like us.

I wished even more that this was not the way things were, even though things did not seem bad. When you hear in the news about neighborhoods where people do not get along, we seem lucky to live in a place like Castle Hill, where so many different kinds of people can be at peace with one another. But meeting Molly made me understand less why the people in our neighborhood could be at once together but still be divided. We could eat each other's food and paint each other's nails, but we did not go to each other's homes or learn each other's language. Why did we settle? I didn't only feel sorry for Molly, who was just like the black fish at Great Wall, swimming without a school in her own tank. I felt bad for all of us, tetras and catfish, too.

I managed to slip back into my room without waking my mother. I crawled into bed without changing from my T-shirt and shorts. I couldn't fall asleep, so I texted Lexi.

QueenNicki: U got in OK?

She never answered because her mother caught her sneaking into the apartment. Lexi never told her just how far she went that night, and she never mentioned that I was with her. Her mother put her on punishment for the rest of the summer. Lexi wasn't even allowed to go outside no matter how hot it got. I would sit on the stoop of our building and text her.

Lexiwithani: Go 2 da park or da movies or sumthin n txt me fm there. Nic u livin 4 us both now!!!!!

I used to be afraid to go to those places without Lexi, and I didn't even understand why. But after our Great Wall adventure, the fear was gone, so I wondered if maybe the ride to Astoria broke me of the spell of together-but-divided that had been cast somehow over our neighborhood. Now I only hesitated because I felt guilty leaving Lexi behind while she was on punishment. I never would have gotten over my fear if not for her. She was my spell-breaker, so it didn't seem fair. This is one of the downsides of having only one BFF, even a magical one like Lexi, who never came under the spell in the first place.

Then one day I was on the stoop texting Lexi about an argument that Marcia was having with her boyfriend when I saw someone coming toward me on a bike. It was Molly. "What's up?" she said, stopping her bike at my foot.

"Hey." She handed me a paper bag. "I didn't order anything."

"I know. It's for you and Lexi with an *i*," said Molly. "Haven't been to the restaurant in a while."

"Yeah, 'cause I'm broke and Lexi's grounded."

"Me too, if I don't finish these deliveries. Had to bribe Pete to let me do them, too, 'cause if my parents knew I was doing them instead of him, it'd be both our hides." I wanted to ask her why her parents didn't want to let her do deliveries, but Molly hopped back on her bike. "But I'll come through on my way back to the restaurant."

And that's when I knew that I would have plenty of chances to ask Molly that question and more. "Cool. And thanks!" And just like that, she was gone again. On the order slip stapled to the bag, Molly had written her cell phone number. When I opened the bag, I found two egg rolls, a pint of pork fried rice and some fortune cookies. I broke open one of the cookies, and the fortune read, *Your greatest fortune are your friends.* I popped the cookie in my mouth and took out my cell phone.

QueenNicki: Yo! U not gonna believe this . . .

KAREN HESSE

NELL

I am dying. I have been dying for a hundred years. I fear I will always be dying.

In the beginning it pleased me to be on the verge of death, always escaping at the last moment from one body to another. But now . . . now I wish I could stop. Always is a long time.

And I am always a child. Always twelve. I've told so many lies. I've taken the identities of so many children. But I think I was born once in the usual way to a man and a woman and the woman died and I was expected to die, too. But I didn't. I don't know why.

I survived to the age of twelve. It was a miserable life, that first one. If I can trust my memory at all, it was a life of hunger and pain, a lonely life, with a father who treated me like dung on the heel of his boot. Even before I could speak, he sent me out to beg. On the days I brought nothing home, he would beat me until I turned to fog and lifted out of my body. I think that's how it began, how I learned to jump.

One winter night in my twelfth year, my father hit me and hit me and did not stop. Once again I felt myself transformed into mist, but this time, when the mist faded, I was inside another body. She had been ill, the girl whose body I *now* inhabited. But she was gone and I was there. What happened to her I don't know. What happened to my first body I cannot say. But I learned quickly to adapt to a new life.

And I learned to prolong that life for months, though never for more than a year. And that's how it continues. The children whose bodies I take are always twelve. I keep them alive as long as I can. But sometime during the year their bodies fail and I lift out of one and slip into another.

I am always dying. I am never dying. I have died and died and died again, but I do not stay dead.

Tonight another twelfth year ends. This time I am an only child, adored by my parents. Of all the parents I have known, these are the kindest. Over the years some could ill afford a sick child; others grew weary of caring for one. In public they feigned love but in private they lost patience. I regret that at times I, too, lost my temper with them.

This time is different. In the twelve months I have been here, these parents have never faltered in their devotion. Never have I longed to remain as I long to remain here. And it feels as if I *could* remain.

I am so much healthier than when I first woke in this body. And so beautifully cared for. I sleep on soft sheets in cloudlike comfort. My mother brings the scent of lilacs with her when she leans in to kiss me, which she does frequently. Her tenderness elicits such a response. It amazes me to feel myself rise to her love. And my father, he's so kind. Every day he comes with a present in his pocket. They have spared no expense in finding a cure for me. They have thrown both their energies and their resources into meeting with anyone reputedly wise in the healing arts. Yet they've never subjected me to treatments that might cause undue pain.

I don't know how they will bear this death.

I don't know how I will bear it, either.

Shutting my door, I take from the shelf a book by the Danish storyteller. The fireplace in my bedroom radiates comfort. Embers make delicate sounds, like fine china splintering. This room, like a princess's chamber, sparkles. The chandelier bends firelight and sends it dancing across the ceiling. There is a table set with buns and cocoa.

In my hands the book falls open to my favorite story. I make my way to the green silk couch with its soft pillows. Curling up, I pull the fur wrapper over my legs, and begin to read . . .

> The Old Year had nearly exhausted itself.
> It slept in a doorway in its worn rags.
> The New Year struggled to be born, locked in the
>   Old Year's embrace.
> Given the state of its decline, the Old Year held back the
>   New with astonishing vigor.

Sounds of the living reach my ears. A group of holiday revelers, emboldened with drink, defy the storm, shouting to each other on the street beneath my window. My parents host a small dinner party below. I have already put in my appearance. Tomorrow the guests will be shocked to learn of my death.

"But she looked so well," they will say.

"She seemed so much stronger."

On this last day of the Old Year
every living thing bowed to the cold,
the cruel cold,
with its blue light,
with its white fangs.
The cold hovered over the town
like some prehistoric beast.
It beat its wings,
creating eddies of razor-sharp air.

I set the book gently aside, rise, and add more sticks to the fire to counter the cold buffeting the windows. I hear the clock strike eleven before I've settled back onto the couch again.

Snow swirled in the cold wind,
not gentle snow-globe snow
but harsh sandpaper snow,
leaving painful red marks on winter-thin skin.
In the gathering dark, snow sprang, brutish,
lashing out at travelers as they passed,
slicing at the gloom with its fierce claws.

How strange, how very strange to have the weather of this story so closely mirror the weather outside my windows. The wind roars like an enraged animal tonight. It reminds me of lions at the zoo.

How many times have these parents taken me to the zoo? In the summer we would go with a picnic hamper. Mother would make certain my straw hat, with its blue velvet ribbons, kept the sun off my face. I remember insisting I could run down the hill and then, halfway down, collapsing. I had been carrying a choc-olate bun that flew from my hands. Father gathered me in his arms. I nestled into him. He smelled of cologne and freshly pressed cotton. His beard tickled my cheek. He bought me a new bun and held me as I ate it.

I remember watching that day the caged lions pacing in their enclosures. They stopped and studied me, scenting the air. Now it seems as if those lions have escaped. They pace outside my windows, rattling the panes with their deep growls.

One of those travelers, a small girl,
slipped almost invisibly through the masses.
She had no covering for her head.
People moved around her like
packs of lumbering bears wrapped in their brown furs.

I rise from the couch, cross the room to the front windows, and look down. It is hard to see anything through the heavy snow. Just a jostling of figures brown and black and bulky in their winter clothing. Bears. Yes, they look exactly like that. A sea of bears ebbing and flowing beneath my windows. But there is no small girl to be seen.

Of course there isn't. What did I think? I sigh and go back to

my seat, pull the fur blanket up. I have taken a chill from standing at the window, straining to see a girl who exists only in the
pages of a book, only in my imagination.

> The girl had neither hat, nor coat, nor gloves, nor even
>   shoes for her small feet.
> That morning she had stepped into her grandmother's boots.
> But while racing across a busy avenue
> where a carriage steered menacingly toward her,
> the girl had fallen and lost her boots.
> One had been snatched by a boy who told her he would
> use the boot as a sailing boat and go to sea in it.
> He ran off laughing at the girl who stared at him, numb
>   and blinking.
> The other boot had been thrown into the air, landing
> where the girl could not find it
> no matter how she searched.

I have known boys like the one who took the match girl's boot.
Boys whose greatest pleasure arose from tormenting others.
But not in this life. I have known no one like that in this life.
These parents would not allow such a child near me.

> The cold painted its colors on the girl's bare skin.
> Red, blue, white.
> These colors dappled her thin arms and legs, but most
>   vividly, they made a startling pattern on her feet.

Lifting the fur wrap, I stretch out my own foot. On it is a silk stocking and a white silk slipper. Slowly, I uncover my foot until it is bare. Holding it up before the firelight, it looks warm, pink, healthy. The scent of talcum fills my nostrils.

> Her soiled apron had a pocket across the front, but the
>   stitching had let go.
> Anything placed inside the pocket instantly fell to the ground.
> So the girl held her apron lifted in such a way as to cradle
>   the matches she had for sale.

Stirring in my mind is this memory: I, too, had been sent out with no coat, no covering, no protection from the elements. I, too, had been careful not to lose my wares, the fragile flowers I had picked the summer before and hung upside down so they might retain some color when they dried. But who wanted such dead brown things? Only those who felt pity gave me money for my bouquets.

But there were days when no one felt charitable toward me and I would come home hungry and empty-handed and then my father, yes, I remember, my father would beat me. And I would have bruises that looked like the mottling of my skin from the cold so that you could not tell where my father's cruelty left off and the cruelty of nature took over.

> This had not been a good day for the girl.
> The cold made people blindly plow past in their coats and
>   shawls,

shoulders hunched, eyes squinted against the stinging flakes.
They did not see the girl with her apron folded up under her
    chin, trying to keep her matchsticks from escaping.
Or if they saw, they did not stop and fish out a coin for her.

I restore the stocking and slipper to my foot, pull the fur wrap
up to my chin.

How she shivered.
How her mouth watered with longing when she passed a
    rosy-cheeked boy eating a bun,
soiling his mitten with bakery grease,
dropping crumbs and bits of raisins in his wake,
ignoring the admonitions of his father,
who held on tightly to keep the boy from running into the
    people around him.
The match girl stopped walking and stood where the bun-eater
    had stood and drew in a deep breath,
devouring the scent of the sweet roll that still lingered in
    the cold air.

I hear a cry from the street. It sounds more like a kitten mewl-
ing than a human voice, especially coming in the midst of bells
jangling, horses clopping, winds whipping, voices calling out to
each other. I hear a cry, a weak cry. "Matches," it says.
"Matches." I must be imagining it from the book. But how real
it sounds.

What a sight she made,

pale and trembling,

exposed to the rude manners of the cold.

Snow gathered in her hair, turning it from blond to white,

covering the long curls with a lacy snow scarf.

If someone had looked carefully at her, they might have thought

under the grime and misery

great beauty resided.

But no one looked carefully at her.

No one noticed her at all.

She was of no matter, not even to herself.

A powerful force lifts me to my feet. Gripping the book, I hurry
to the window.

As she passed before the shops, yellow light spilled into
    the street.

Every kind of luxury could be found there.

Bright silken fabrics, a cobbler who made slippers of the
    softest leather, a cafe, a shop that sold fine silver.

On the second and third and fourth floors, above
    the shops, people moved in their lighted apartments.

The sound of music came softly through their windows, and
    laughter, and the heavenly aroma of roasted meat.

The girl looked up to see a child looking down at her from
    one of the upper stories.

For a moment their eyes met and the match girl felt herself
    being lifted.

But then an oafish man trod on her and the match girl felt
with renewed pain the unbearable coldness of her feet.

And I see her. She exists. She is there below me, outside my
window.

I want to bring her up out of the storm, to bring her into my
bedroom where I can warm her.

A crowd of revelers passes the match girl, blocking her from
my sight. When they move on, she has vanished. I am desperate
to find her but she is gone.

Between the bookseller's shop and the shop that sold confec-
tions, a recessed doorway offered shelter to the little match girl.
She pressed the thin bones of her back against the wood of the
door and imagined the heat from inside the building.
Protected here, she could not be so fiercely bitten by the wind.
No one could see her and so she could make no sales,
but here at least the snow could not tear at her.

I scan the doorways, seeking her. Even though I have not seen
her go, I suspect she, too, like the child in the story, has sought
a doorway for shelter. And yes, there is movement in the
shadows. As if a small animal circled and settled there, seeking
comfort.

I must stop my trembling. If there is any chance of prolong-
ing this life, I must tear myself from the bitter draft at the window. I carry the storybook to the hearth, and stand before the
fire.

She would be content to stay here and never go home.
At home only her father waited, like a monster,
with his hot temper and his stinging blows.
She had not a single coin to give him and that would stir
    his anger to boiling.
He would beat her.
She knew that with certainty.
He would beat her savagely.
No, she would not go home.
She would sit in this sheltered doorway forever.

The fire warms me. I feel its soothing touch. The warmth enters my hands, toasts my face, raises the temperature of the book.

She peered out from her arch of protection.
Everywhere she saw the golden glow of the town.
She held her small hands up toward the lighted windows
but she was beyond the reach of their comfort.

I can't leave her out there. I can't let her go on that way. No matter what it costs me, I must bring her here, to me, bring her into this room, talk to her, warm her, comfort her.

The match girl sank down, drew herself into a ragged bundle.
Perhaps, tucked in like this, she was small enough to be
    warmed by the fire of one of her own matches.
If she lit it, she would be a penny poorer.
But if she lit it, she would have a penny's worth of warmth.

I shut my eyes and concentrate. I know precisely what she needs, what she wants. I imagine her here in this room with me. I imagine a shaft of light guiding her, her path beginning at the arched doorway and ending just inside my bedroom. I will her to come here, to join me.

She scraped the match against the cold brick wall beside the
    door and a lick of fire sprang up at the stick's end.
Now she had a tiny globe of golden light at her command.
She drank in the dancing blue-orange-white skirt of flame.
A ballet of fire.
She could feel its liquid warmth on her face.
She felt herself being lifted by it into a room where a fireplace
    burned brightly, giving off waves of soothing heat.
She could hear a voice speaking to her from somewhere in
    the room,
but she could not make out the words.
The voice did not sound cruel,
not like the boy who had stolen her boot.
It sounded surprised, breathless, welcoming.

"It's all right," I tell her. "Don't be frightened. Let me help you."

She turned toward the voice and just then the match burned
    itself out and
the girl felt the darkness and cold close back around her.
The tiny stub of a match dropped to the ground from her
    numb fingers.

I had her for a moment. I could see her hair dusted with snow, the blue of her ears, the threadbare fabric of her dress. I held her here for a moment, only a moment. And then she slipped back, back into the book, back outside my window. I must try harder, strain harder to bring her here again.

The cold felt like a stone weight on the match girl's chest.
Struggling against the heaviness, she lit another match.
With a sudden spark, then a whisss, the match blossomed
    into life.
Holding up the lighted match, the girl could see through
    the walls surrounding her,
as if the match turned the brick and wood to glass.
She chose the apartment she wanted to enter, the one with
    the child who had looked down at her from above.
And there was the child. She stood in a beautiful bedroom in
    which a small table held court on its sturdy four legs,
    bearing on its white cloth back a perfectly polished silver
    tray of sweet buns and a sparkling pot of chocolate.
A delicate china bowl held an array of ripe fruit.
The smells thrilled the match girl's nose and made her mouth
    fill eagerly with hope.
The child pulled out a chair and beckoned for the match girl
    to sit.
But then the flame from the match reached the girl's fingertips,
    too cold to feel the singe before the flame died.
And once again she huddled deep into the recess of the
    doorway, in the hungry dark.

"Come back. Please come back. I can give this to you. I can give this all to you. You must help me, though. You must want it too. Concentrate. Come back."

She struck a third match.
Instantly she was back inside the apartment with the child.

The match girl stands before me. Her eyes widen as she looks at the chandelier, the table laden with food, the enormous gilded mirror. Her eyes fix on the Christmas tree. It sparkles with glass baubles. Light from the fire dances the tree's shadow up and down the wall. The boughs scent my room with the spicy aroma of pine.

The girl had never been inside a room like this.
A crystal chandelier twinkled like a constellation of stars.
The match girl smelled a dizzying perfume.

She moves awkwardly on her frozen feet, half teeter, half stumble. I go to her and hold her hand. She wants to touch the tree, to examine the decorations.

Paintings adorned the walls.
The child who had called her took her hand and they stood
    together.
And the third match reached its end.
When the girl looked up, the place where the chandelier
    had hung was filled with stars.
The snow had stopped falling and the sky had cleared.

> The cold was the fiercest it had been all day.
> But with her eyes turned upward, the girl saw a star shoot
>   across the heavens.
> It traced a path of light.
> It was beautiful the way it made a bright bridge across
>   the sky.

"A shooting star. Someone's fortune will change." That's what I had been told about shooting stars. That when a star left a track of shimmering dust across the sky, someone's fortune would change.

> "Someone's fortune will change," the match girl thought,
> her arms wrapped tightly around her shivering body.
> Her grandmother,
> the only person who had ever loved her,
> had told her so. She had told her a shooting star was an
> omen of change.
> Often of death.

It is *my* fortune that will change. I know it with certainty. *I can go on in this life.* Or I can give this body, this life, to the match girl, by willingly taking her place. The match girl will die this night. I must will myself to enter her dead body and let her take this living one. I will take her death. I will give her this life, for I am certain now this body will go on.

> All at once the girl scratched the remainder of her matches
>   into life.

The glow filled the sheltered doorway and spilled out onto
    the street.
Coming toward her was that beloved child from the room
    above, that angel of comfort.

"What's happening?" the match girl asks.
    "Your name will be Nell," I tell her.

A little crowd in hats and coats and boots
stood gaping at the small frozen body in the doorway
between the bookseller and the confectioner.
The snow around her held the match stubs that she'd lit
    the night before.
The last she had lit at midnight, as the Old Year finally re-
    leased its grip and allowed the New Year to be born.
"It's a wonder she didn't set fire to the building," a woman
    in a purple shawl said.

The match girl looks out from Nell's eyes. She holds the hand
of Nell's mother and the hand of Nell's father and they come
close to the stiff, cold body, because the child says they must.

"We must see to her burial," the match girl says. "We must
see that her body has every comfort it lacked while she lived."

And the parents, who do not know they lost their daughter,
their Nell, once, a year before, and once more, last night, look
adoringly at this child who is alive, who is theirs, and say, "Of
course. Of course. Of course."

GARY SOTO

WHAT I WISH FOR

I make a wish and blow on a tottering candle,
Smoke like a lasso when the flame goes out.

Outside, in the yard,
I busy myself with clippers.
I make another wish: a dandelion explodes.
The wind, I see, flies east,
A cargo of cumulus clouds not far behind.

Before my nap, I make a wish.
Behind my closed eyelids
I see my bedroom tidy itself up—
My food-stained pants on the floor walk themselves
Down the hallway, through the kitchen,
And jump into the washer.

Monday, Tuesday, let's skip Wednesday and go to Thursday,
When the farmers' market pitches its tents.
It's October, good season for apples.
What I really want is a melon big as a wheelbarrow,
But I buy three Fuji apples,
One to eat and the others to juggle
On the way home.

When I toss a nickel into a pond,
A koi surfaces, her mouth throwing out kisses—
I return the kiss with my fingertips.
The koi wiggles its glossy tail and disappears,
A ripple on the surface,
A ripple in my memory.

If only I were a rocker.
I would write a song called "Wishful Thinking,"
A tremendous hit with my three friends
And my jailbird parrot, I should add—
See how he salsas on his trapeze?

But I'm not a rocker.
I have harmless ambitions, secret wishes . . .
If only I could drive a car backwards.
I could chug up a hill in second gear,
My companion in the passenger seat
A hungry goat. When we reach the fire trail,
The goat snacks on a serving of dandelions.

I could visit the sea, too.
Waves slide up the beach, then back,
The crab a fortress in itself,
Its claws like pliers, its eyes like dark periods
Ending sentence fragments.
Yes, this is where I wish
To be, the sea with kelp and seagulls,
Kites going berserk,
And shells the color of baby teeth,
Tokens I could pocket for free.

Under a low sky,
I'll applaud the clouds arriving from China—
The world loves me, the world loves me,
The world most certainly loves me . . .

Overwhelmed with chores, refugee children often miss school.
Photo Credit (both): *UNHCR / M. Collins*

JOHN GREEN

REASONS

REASONS AISHA HUSSAIN IS UNLIKELY TO BEFRIEND ME: A LIST BY MICAH FELDMAN

1. When you look into the huge round eyes of Aisha Hussain, as I do several times a day, you get the sense that she does not want or need a male companion. You get the sense that she is maybe a little bit like a twelve-year-old version of Gloria Steinem, who once said that a woman needs a man like a fish needs a bicycle. The eyes of Aisha Hussain say, you know, "Everything I will ever need to be happy is already here, swimming inside my eye sockets." It's very impressive.

2. Aisha Hussain is not aware that I exist. It could be argued that this is advantageous, since certainly none of the girls who *do* know I exist are particularly fond of me, but still.

3. My mom thinks there is a reasonably high chance that Aisha Hussain is fictional, or at least that she is a cobbled-together phenomenon.
4. In the unlikely event that Aisha Hussain were ever to be a fish in need of a bicycle, I would be a poor candidate.

THINGS AISHA HUSSAIN MIGHT ADMIRE IN A GUY: A LIST BY MICAH FELDMAN

1. Physical strength: One time in fourth grade my teacher Mr. Farnsworth, who was not technically what you would consider a very nice man, was trying to explain to us the difference between conditional tenses in English, and he pointed out that the sentence "Micah Feldman can do a pull-up" is *always* untrue, whereas the sentence "Micah Feldman *could* do a pull-up" might be true, depending on whether the sentence ended with "if he ate his Wheaties." (I do eat my Wheaties, by the way. If Aisha Hussain is looking for a Wheaties eater, I am her man.)
2. Economic status: Living, as she does, in the disputed region of Kashmir, on an income of less that one dollar a day, presumably Aisha Hussain would be impressed with a young man who could deliver a solid wage. On this front, I have at least a chance: The reason I know Aisha Hussain in the first place is that Mom is sponsoring her. Mom sends sixty dollars a month to For The Children, and then For The Children gets food for Aisha Hussain. Also other stuff, like this month she got some shoes. She'd never had shoes before. She was pretty psyched about it, according to her letter. (Aisha sends us a letter

each month, but it's typewritten, and Mom thinks that
Aisha Hussain doesn't actually write the letters, and that
in fact she probably *can't* write due to the poor female
education in the disputed region of Kashmir.) Anyway, I
have economic status insofar as my mom has sixty spare
dollars to send to Kashmir every month, but I do not
have particularly good economic prospects personally.
For instance, it would cost about $3,460 to get to Aisha's
village, and my current net worth is $337.43, money
made from a fledgling lawn-care business.

3. Badness: Lately, I have been watching a number of Bollywood films, which are like regular movies except a) they
   are not in English and b) there is quite a bit more dancing.
   And if I have learned one thing from Bollywood movies,
   it is that people who live on the Indian subcontinent want
   their boys to be at least Slightly Bad, which is a lot like
   girls in America, and unfortunately, I am really bad at
   being bad. Like, I can break rules and stuff—I can sneak
   out my window and go outside after curfew—but doing it
   makes me feel very *nervous,* and so when I am being bad,
   I can never look suitably nonchalant about it. Also, I
   cannot dance, which is another requirement of romantic
   leads, at least according to these Bollywood movies I have
   been watching. I mean, I guess technically I can dance in
   the sense that my body is able to move, but when I move
   my body while music is playing, anyone watching
   inevitably says, "Wow, you *really cannot dance,*" which
   generally stops me dead in my tracks.

THINGS MY MOTHER CITED WHEN CONFRONTING ME ABOUT MY FASCINATION WITH AISHA HUSSAIN: A LIST BY MICAH FELDMAN

1. My desire to get the mail. Every day I come home from school and I get off the bus and I get the mail and bring it inside to Mom. As she pointed out, I only started doing this after Aisha Hussain entered our lives, almost as if I only check the mail to see if one of Aisha's typewritten notes has arrived.

2. The whole Bollywood movie fascination.

3. My insistence when participating in my school's Model United Nations club that I represent either India or Pakistan, and my obsessive submission of resolutions involving the disputed region of Kashmir.

4. The fact that the only picture of Aisha we have ever received—a picture which Mom intentionally threw away because such pictures are only attempts to tug on your heartstrings and which I, she correctly guessed, rescued from the trash—is pinned to the corkboard in my bedroom over my desk, which Mom discovered even though the picture in question is almost entirely hidden by an honor roll certificate from Glenridge Middle School.

5. A review of my Web browsing history, which by the way was a complete invasion of my privacy, turned up extensive research into the subject of how to fly to the disputed region of Kashmir.

6. Decreased interest in real-world social interactions, including a total lack of Visits From Friends.

RESPONSES TO MY MOTHER'S CONFRONTATION,
WHICH HAPPENED ON THE WHITE COUCH OF OUR LIVING
ROOM, WITH MOM AND I STARTING OUT ON OPPOSITE SIDES
OF THE COUCH BUT THEN THROUGHOUT HER
CONFRONTATION AND MY RESPONSE SHE KEPT SCOOTING
TOWARD ME AND EVENTUALLY ASKED ME IF I NEEDED A
CUDDLE, WHICH, LIKE, NO, I MEAN, I AM TWELVE YEARS
OLD, MOM, I DO NOT NEED CUDDLES FROM MOTHERS:
A LIST BY MICAH FELDMAN

1. To be fair, I never had friends. It's not fair to blame my
   friendlessness on a thirteen-year-old girl who lives 11,451
   miles away from me.
2. Anyone who has ever watched an entire Bollywood movie
   has found the experience utterly and totally delightful,
   including you, Mom.
3. I cannot be held responsible for the fact that Aisha Hussain
   has truly arresting eyes, and it's important when sitting at
   my desk doing my homework occasionally to be reminded
   that there are people for whom going to school is not an
   unbearable burden but instead an exciting opportunity.
4. The future of the disputed region of Kashmir is an
   important geopolitical issue not only to people who
   sponsor Aisha Hussain through For The Children but also
   to any informed citizen of the world, given that both India
   and Pakistan are nuclear powers and everything.
5. All that said, in the interest of full disclosure it should
   probably be noted that I have been sending Aisha Hussain
   money.

Some Questions My Mother Had re Aisha and the Money:
A List by Micah Feldman

1. What?
2. How much?
3. How?
4. Are you crazy?
5. Have you been taking your medication?
6. Do you think this girl cares about you or knows who you are or wants anything other than your money? Or do you even think that she's real? Don't you realize that your money is probably being intercepted along the way and never even gets to her, if she's even real, which she probably isn't, because these organizations "sponsor" tens of thousands of kids and only pick the attractive ones to put on the postcards because then you'll send more money? Don't you understand it's just advertising, Micah? She's not *real*.

Some Answers:
A List by Micah Feldman

1. I have been sending her money.
2. So far about $337. Mowing money.
3. I put it in an envelope and I mailed it to her village with her name on it. I did it at school. Mrs. Yeovil at the front office, she has this machine that will figure out how much it costs to mail anything anywhere.
4. I am not crazy, but I have issues with socialization, as you are well aware, that have been extensively documented.
5. Yes.

6. I don't know if she cares about me. I don't know if she'll
    ever get the money. But she is real, Mom. She has a
    picture. You can't make up a picture.

SOME EXAMPLES OF PHOTOGRAPHS
NOT ACTUALLY BEING PARTICULARLY PHOTOGRAPHIC:
A LIST BY MY MOTHER

1. You've seen those airbrushed celebrities on magazine
    covers, Micah. Are not those pictures made up?
2. Did you know in fact that the staging of photographs is as
    old as photography itself? When Mathew Brady took
    pictures of Civil War dead in the 1860s, he would drag
    their bodies around to give them the most dramatic
    possible death poses.
3. In fact, if you really think about it, all photographs are
    doctored because there is always a choice about what goes
    in the shot and what doesn't. Even if that girl is real, they
    probably washed her and put her in front of the ideally
    impoverished background, Micah.
4. The job of that photograph is to make you like that girl so
    you send the charity sixty dollars a month. I send them
    sixty dollars not because of that girl but because they're a
    reputable organization known for spending money
    efficiently to address poverty and disease in the developing
    world, Micah, you understand that? That's why I tossed
    the photograph the moment it arrived and why I've taken
    the liberty of removing it from your corkboard. You
    cannot be swayed by a photograph. You don't choose
    charities based on the quality of their photography, Micah.

Don't you think your $337 would have been better spent saving lives through the purchase of mosquito nets for— Micah? Are you crying?

Reasons I Was Crying:
A List by Micah Feldman

1. It was the only picture I had of Aisha and the only image I would probably ever see of her. Even if she received the $337, and even if she was grateful and wrote me back, she probably couldn't include a picture because she probably didn't have a camera, given that she recently received her first-ever pair of shoes and whatnot. I thought about including a camera in the envelope with the $337, but a) it would have been much more expensive to mail, according to Mrs. Yeovil at the front office, and b) I guess it's probably a little creepy to receive $337 and a camera from a stranger, like far creepier than just receiving $337.

2. Why can't you just be allowed to believe that someone is real if you want to and not be told by your mom that you are an idiot and wasted your life savings? I wish it could be like it was when I was littler, when I was allowed to just *believe* things and no one would get mad at me.

3. I want Aisha Hussain to exist. I want her to be real and to be pretty and round-eyed, and I want whatever our cultural differences may be to be surmountable, and I want us to be friends. I don't want photographs to be nonphotographic. I don't want the kind of mother who points out things like that, instead of just letting me like Aisha Hussain from the magnificently safe distance of 11,451 miles.

WHAT I WISHED FOR THAT NIGHT:
A LIST BY MICAH FELDMAN

1. I cannot tell you or else it won't come true.

And then I was not twelve anymore. I was thirteen, and it
was the summer between seventh and eighth grade, and I had
a bunch of friends on the Internet whom I played this game
with, and it was a pretty good summer, but I still thought of her
every night, thought about how it was not night for her when
it was night for me but how we still looked up at the same sky
at the same time, how every night I would see the stars that she
had seen a few hours earlier, the very same stars, and one afternoon Mom came in and stood between me and the TV screen
and I said, "Mom, I'm on a *mission,*" and she held up an envelope with quite a lot of stamps.

I opened it carefully, the way Mom opens presents when she
wants to save the wrapping paper.

The note inside was written in the Urdu language. I recognized it even though I couldn't read it.

جناب میقہ فلڈم‌ᵇᵃن

پ کے خط کا شکریہ ۔ آپ نے کہا ہے کہ آپ نے پیسے بھیجے ہیں لیکن
میں نے آپ کو بتانا ہے . وہ نہیں ملا ۔ یہاں پیسے بھیجنے کے لئے ڈاک
کا ذریعہ اچھا نہیں ہے ۔ کیا امریکا میں یہ اچھا طریقہ ہے؟ آپ کا خط
ملا جس سے مجھے بہت خوشی ہواᵇᵃ۔ یہ ہمارے لئےبہت عجیب ہے کہ
آپ کھاس کائنے کا کام کرتے ہیں۔ کیاآپ مشین کو خود دھکیلتے ہیں؟
کیا یہ خطرناک ہے؟ یہاں پیسے بنانے سب سے اچھا طریقہ ہینڈی
کرافٹ ہے۔ کُچھ بچے بس صاف کرنے یا پٹرول سٹیشن میں کام کرتے

میں۔ لیکن ہمارے گھر میں یہ نہیں کرنے دیا جاتا۔ لیکن میرے پاس کام
ہے۔ میں تصویریں بناتی ہوں۔ میں نے ایک اس خط کے ساتھ لفافے
میں ڈالی ہے۔ شاید آپ اپنے جواب میں کچھ گھاس جو آپ کاٹا ہے
مجھے بھیجے سکیں گے۔ اگر آپ جواب دینا چاہیں تو۔ آپ کے خط سے
بہت خوشی ہوئی۔

منجانب عائش،

It said:

Dear Mr. Micah Feldman,

Thank you for your letter. You mention that you sent money, but I must tell you, if you were being serious, it did not arrive. The mail is not a good way to send money here; is it a good way in America? But anyway, your letter did arrive, and it made me very happy. It is very funny to us that you work at grass cutting. Do you push the machine yourself? Is it dangerous? Here the best way to make money is handicrafts. Some kids work as bus cleaners or at fuel stations, but at our home that is not allowed. But I do have a job: I make drawings. I have enclosed one in this note. Perhaps in your reply, you could send me some of the grass you have cut. If you wish to reply, that is.

I hope you will write again anyway. It is very nice to hear from you.

Yours,
Aisha

The drawing was a self-portrait—more beautiful by far than any photograph could have been.

*The author is deeply indebted to Iram Qureshi and Anwar Iqbal for their Urdu translation.

Classrooms are open to sandstorms and deteriorate from seasonal rain.
Photo Credit (both): *UNHCR / H. Caux*

ANN M. MARTIN

THE LOST ART
OF LETTER WRITING

September 14
Dear Jenny,

Hi. My name is Alice Kendall and I'm writing to you because my teacher is weird. Mr. Jessop has only been my teacher for a week and a half and already he's told my class that 1) computers are turning teenagers into couch potatoes who lack social graces, 2) thanks to e-mail, letter writing is becoming a lost art, and 3) Velcro is the reason children can't tie their shoes. I didn't know the Velcro thing was a problem, but whatever. Anyway, getting back to letter writing, that's why I'm writing to you now. Apparently, my teacher knows your teacher, and Mr. Jessop decided that my classmates and I should practice the art of letter writing—on you and your classmates. (Sorry about that.)

So . . . I don't know. Did your teacher tell you the same thing? That it would be all tragic if you didn't know how to write real letters? There were tears in Mr. Jessop's eyes when he said that letter writing is becoming a lost art. Well, okay, I'm exaggerating, but he did have to stop and clear his throat in the middle of the sentence, like, "Blah, blah, blah, and because everyone communicates via e-mail these days, letter writing is becoming," ahem, AHEM, "a lost art."

After that, Mr. Jessop passed around a hat and I drew your name out of it. Jennifer Harris. You are now officially my pen pal. Which means that you should know a few things about me. I'm in eighth grade. I go to Wentworth Academy in Newtown, Connecticut, but I live in Burton, which is about fifteen miles from Newtown. The people in my family are my mom and my dad, my sister Missy, who's ten, and my brother Justin, who's seven. And a bunch of animals.

This is what I know so far about you: You're in eighth grade too, and you go to Lincoln Middle School in Castleton, Ohio, which is a pretty big city. Your school doesn't have a lot of funding and is short on supplies and books and computers, and also needs repairs. I'm really sorry about that. Maybe our class could organize a drive to collect stuff for your class.

I just reread what I've written and I really hope Mr. Jessop isn't going to look at our letters before he sends them to your teacher. I don't want him to see what I said about him. Oh, well. It's too late to change anything now.

He's about to collect our papers. Unlike with e-mail, I can't go back and delete stuff. If letter writing is an art, so far its decline doesn't seem like much of a loss. I'm going to seal this up before Mr. Jessop gets his hands on it.

Hastily,
Alice Kendall

~~~~~~~~~~~~~~~~~~~~~~~~~~~~~~~~~~~~~~~

September 21
Dear Alice,

First of all, my name is Jennifer, not Jenny. And second of all, my school doesn't need any help. We're doing fine. But I guess it was nice of you to offer.

Yes, our teachers know each other, but mine didn't say anything about the lost art of letter writing. Maybe that's because hardly anybody in my class has a computer at home, and the ones at school are from, like, the 1900s, so there's no danger of losing the art of letter writing here in Castleton. All my teacher said was that we were getting pen pals for the semester. My teacher's name is Ms. Dennis, by the way, and I was lucky to wind up in her class. A lot of kids don't like her. They think she's strict. But I think she's fair. (I don't like teachers who let their students get away with stuff.)

So here are some things about me: I live with my father, my grandparents (Dad's parents), my sister Ava (she's 15), and my cousins who are twins but not identical. They're 16 and their names are Pat and Chris. I'll leave it up to you to figure out if they're boys or girls or one of each. Ha, ha.

You said you live with a lot of animals. I assume you mean pets. We don't have any pets because they're too expensive. That's also why we don't have a computer. If my dad got a job we might adopt a cat, but that doesn't look too promising. I mean, the possibility of his finding a job doesn't look too promising. Right now my grandmother is the only one who earns any money. Oh, and also Chris delivers papers in the a.m. before school. And in case you're thinking I just gave you a clue, remember that boys aren't the only ones who can have paper routes.

My dad is an inventor but he hasn't invented anything good in ages, which is why we had to move in with my grandparents. What do your parents do?

Also, is Wentworth Academy a private school? It must be, with a name like that and a teacher who's concerned about the lost art of letter writing. I've never known anyone who went to a private school.

Well, Ms. Dennis just gave us five more minutes to finish our letters, so I'd better stop here. I hope you can read my handwriting okay. Chris says it's stupid to dot my i's with flowers, but I think the flowers say something about my cheerful personality. Ha, ha.

Sincerely,

Jennifer Harris

P.S. The kids at my school may not be rich, but don't read too much into that.

September 30
Dear Jennifer,

If you're going to be picky, then please call me Allie.
That's my nickname, although I don't get all huffy if
people call me Alice. Also, I do go to a private school, but
talk about assumptions—you shouldn't read too much into
the subject of Wentworth Academy. I'll get back to
assumptions and my school later, though.

First things first, I'm sorry if I offended you by
offering to help your class. It's just something I do. I
mean, thinking up ways to help people is something I do.
Well, actually, offending people is something I do too, but
not on purpose. I can be a little pushy. My friend Lucinda
says I go overboard with helpfulness. She's getting tired
of bake sales and clothing drives and collection cans, and
also of sticking up for me every time I put my foot in my
mouth. And I can't blame her. Luckily, we've been friends
since we were three. Well, anyway, I'm sorry. I won't bring
up the subject of a drive again.

As for Wentworth, my sister and brother and I go here
because my father teaches one of the fourth-grade
classes, so we get scholarships. Otherwise, my parents
couldn't afford the tuition. So don't you go reading too
much into my life, okay? (FYI, my mother is a part-time
bookkeeper in Burton.)

All right. Let's go to a different subject. I'll tell you
about our animals. We live way out in the country and we

have two dogs and one cat, and my brother has a ferret named Harriet. (He thinks "ferret" and "Harriet" rhyme.) Also, we see tons of animals in our yard and in the woods. Here's a partial list: coyotes, foxes (gray and red), raccoons, skunks, squirrels (black, gray, and red), mice, bats, deer, woodchucks, weasels, snakes, turtles, lots of different kinds of birds, and . . . bears. No kidding. We really do see bears. Needless to say, our cat doesn't go outdoors, even though he would like to.

Okay, about Pat and Chris, I guess you're going to keep giving me clues about them. That will be fun. Can I just ask one question, though? How come they live with you? (If that's too nosy, you don't have to answer. I tend to be nosy in addition to offensive and pushy.)

I have a fun idea. In your next letter, why don't you tell me ten interesting things about yourself, okay?

Sincerely,

Allie

P.S. Let's try to stop being aggravated with each other.

P.P.S. Mr. Jessop never looks at our letters. We seal them in envelopes before we give them to him. He said Ms. Dennis doesn't look at your letters either. So we can quit worrying that they'll see what we've written. They just want us to experience letter writing.

October 9
Dear Allie,

Okay, I guess I had that coming. About assumptions, I mean. So . . . I'm sorry. And, okay, let's try not to be aggravated with each other. Maybe we should just start over.

Hi, my name is Jennifer. Here are ten things about me. I hope you think they're interesting:

1. The best gadget my father ever invented was this light-up magnifying glass for old people to use when they can't read the menu in a restaurant—and then it turned out that someone else had already invented it. That was right before we moved in with my grandparents.

2. My best subject in school is English and Ms. Dennis says I'm a very good writer. I like to write, and I know Ms. Dennis kind of hopes I'll become a writer one day, but I haven't thought that far ahead. I just know I want to go to college.

3. One of my cousins is pregnant. So now you know that at least one of them is a girl, but I'm not going to tell you which one. The baby is due next month—and our house is already pretty crowded. . . .

4. My mom died when I was four. She had a heart attack, which the doctors said was unlucky at her age. If you ask me, it's unlucky at any age.

5. I do think you're a little nosy, but I don't mind. About my cousins—they don't live with us, we live with them. I

mean, when we moved in with my grandparents, they were
already here. Nannie and Poppy have raised them since
they were babies and were taken away from their parents.
(Their mother is my father's sister.) Nobody really talks
about why they got taken away. I once heard my father
say that they're troubled.

6. I like to collect stuff and save stuff, which is not
easy in a house like mine where there isn't much space.
There are three small bedrooms in my grandparents' house.
Nannie and Poppy have one, my sister and I have one, and
my cousins share the third. Dad sleeps in the living room.
After my cousin's baby comes, she and the baby will get
one room to themselves, and my other cousin will move in
with my sister and me. So anyway, I have to collect things
that are both small and free, like pictures of people with
unfortunate hairdos.

7. I stole all my cousin's money (the cousin who's having
the baby). This is because Brandon (that's the baby's
father) has some weird power over her, and she doesn't
seem to have a mind of her own when he's around. She's
been earning $$ to pay for the baby's expenses, and she has
a lot saved, but all Brandon has to do is ask for it—which I
know he'll do eventually—and she'll fork it over in one
second. Brandon is 22 and has a drinking problem, so I
know exactly how he'll spend a load of cash. I'll give the
$$ back to my cousin after the baby is born and she finds
out how expensive diapers are.

8. I'm afraid of clowns and moths.

9. The farthest I've ever traveled is Cleveland.

10. I have a secret best friend. Her name is Starla.
Sincerely,
Jennifer

~~~~~~~~~~~~~~~~~~~~~~~~~~~~~

October 13
11:15 p.m., so obviously not written in class
Dear Jennifer,

Hey, wait a minute! How can you just end your letter
by saying you have a <u>secret</u> best friend—with a name as
interesting as Starla? You have to ~~elaba ellab~~ tell me
more. That is all for now.

> Your intrigued friend,
> Allie

P.S. I just realized that both your cousins are girls,
right? Because if they're sharing a room, and if the one
who isn't having the baby is going to move in with you and
your sister, then she must be a girl too. Now the only
question is, which one is Pat and which one is Chris?

~~~~~~~~~~~~~~~~~~~~~~~~~~~~~

October 20
4:20 p.m.—not written in class either. You're about to
find out where I am.
Dear Allie,

That was pretty clever of you to figure out that my
cousins are both girls. And since you've already figured out

the main part, I'll tell you that Pat is the one who's going to have the baby, which by the way is a boy, and Chris, the one who makes fun of my handwriting, is the one who will be moving in with Ava and me. The three of us are going to be crowded, that's for sure. Ava and Chris are each going to get one of the bunk beds, and I'll be sleeping on a fold-up cot that we can put away during the day. In case you're wondering, the reason Chris gets the bunk bed is because she and Pat lived here first. And she's older. Dad tried to stick up for me when my grandparents made the decision about the bedrooms, but the truth is that no one wants to share a room with an infant, except for Pat, who has no choice. And I don't really care whether I sleep on a cot or on the bottom bunk.

Ha! I knew that #10 on the list would get to you. And I guess I could be really mean and end my letter here, but I won't do that. Here is the story of Starla. It starts with wishes:

I wish for a lot of things, like a room of my own, and some privacy, and that Dad would invent something really popular (and original), and that Chris wouldn't make fun of me all the time. She torments me for getting good grades and for staying out of trouble (she's jealous), and she calls me Pinocchio—not because I lie (that's <u>her</u> specialty), but because of the size of my nose. Anyway, most of all, I wish I had a best friend. Well, I used to wish for that, and then I met this really cool girl and her name was Starla and that seemed like fate. Because of her name. <u>Starla</u>. And I was <u>wishing</u>. Get it? Wishing on a star(la)?

As you can imagine, the less time I have to spend at home with Chris, the better. So last summer, every day after I had finished with this baby-sitting job I had, I would go to the Coffee Cup, which is about four blocks away. It's a coffeehouse where I like to hang out. Not that I drink coffee. I just like sitting at the little scarred tables, working on my poems in the dim light. Sometimes there are poetry readings at the Coffee Cup and those are really interesting and so are the poets' outfits and hairdos. Anyway, I would settle down there every afternoon at about 4:00 and this waitress who had the most amazing haircut I'd ever seen would always ask me if I wanted to order something, and I'd always say no, and she never minded. She'd just let me sit and write. Sometimes on her breaks she would sit down with me and ask how I was and what I was working on. Like she was really interested. And she always looked right into my eyes and listened very seriously to my answers. Eventually, Starla and I (Starla is the waitress, in case you couldn't guess) started talking and it turned out that she's only seventeen, but already she has dropped out of school and lives on her own and is supporting herself. Can you imagine? She didn't like the way things were in her home, but unlike me, she did something about it. On the other hand, at her house it wasn't just a matter of overcrowded bedrooms and jealous cousins.

Anyway, Starla and I are kindred spirits. I think she's the only one in the world who understands me. And she <u>wants</u> to understand me. We've become really good friends. Starla lets me come over to her apartment when she isn't working, and she styles my hair and shows me the books she's reading to educate herself since "the traditional educational system has failed her." She never criticizes anything about me, she always wants to hear about school, and she tells me to put Chris's comments out of my head. She says they're useless, that they're hurting my psyche, and that they clutter up my mind. "Fill your mind with the things that matter," she says. Also, she tells me I'm a strong young woman and that I can do anything I want in life. At Starla's, I feel like the most important person in the world.

Wow. It's getting late. I'd better go. I'm enclosing my school picture so you can see what I look like (even though it isn't a very good picture—my nose looks bigger than usual, and my hair doesn't usually have that strange swirl near my right ear). I'm also sending you one of my poems.

Your friend,

Jennifer

~~~~~~~~~~~~~~~~~~~~~~~~~~~~

October 31, aka Halloween

Writing from the Coffee Cup again

Dear Allie,

I haven't heard from you in a while. Is everything okay? I kind of hoped you would write back after I told you about Starla—and sent you my picture and poem. I hope I didn't say something to offend you.

Did I?

—Jennifer

~~~~~~~~~~~~~~~~~~~~~~~~~~~~

November 6

Dear Jennifer,

I'm really sorry I didn't write back sooner. I love having your school picture and the poem. I've saved them with your letters. You don't look a thing like I thought you would. You know how sometimes you create an image of someone based on the way that person sounds over the phone? Well, based on the way you sound on paper, I pictured you as having cool glasses and a very sophisticated hairstyle. I didn't know what color your skin or hair or eyes would be, but I imagined a short haircut, maybe a little spiky on the top, and thick black intellectual glasses. Now I see that you don't wear glasses—at least you're not wearing them in the picture—and although your hair <u>is</u> incredibly sophisticated, it's way different than I had pictured it. How long is it? Does it reach your waist? And, ahem, your nose is not big at all. It's just a nice regular nose. I don't know <u>what</u> Chris is talking about. Starla is right. Chris is probably hurting your psyche.

Your poem is amazing. Thank you for sending it. I don't know anyone who writes poetry like yours.

Well, now I guess I should explain why I've been out of touch. There is a good reason, even though it doesn't excuse me from writing. On October 15th my dad was fired from his job. Well, he wasn't exactly fired, but his position was "eliminated," along with about eight other positions at school, in order to cut costs. The principal, Mrs. Mason, plans to combine the two smaller fourth-grade classes into one big class, so out went Dad. Mrs. Mason said Missy and Justin and I can stay at Wentworth on our scholarships until the end of the semester, but starting in January Mom and Dad will have to pay full tuition. Of course, there's no way they can afford that, especially since less than a week after Dad was fired, Mom was fired from <u>her</u> job. Her boss also said that her position had been "eliminated," but I don't think "eliminated" sounds any better than "fired," do you? I am so mad—and also so sad. Everybody's trying to save money these days, and how do they do it? By taking away people's jobs. Missy and Justin and I will switch to public school in January. But you know what? I wish we could switch right now. At school, everyone knows that Dad got fired and they look at my brother and sister and me with this horrifying mix of pity and disgust—like Dad did something wrong and got caught, and now <u>we're</u> paying for it.

I'm having trouble concentrating on my work.

So that's my sad story. Sharing it with you makes me feel better, though.

I'm enclosing my school picture here so that you can see what I look like. I wonder how you've been picturing me. Oh, I'm also enclosing a photo of Snow White and Sleeping Beauty, our dogs. And before you say anything, I named them when I was six and didn't know any better. They go by Snowy and Beauty.

Love,
Allie

November 8

Dear Jennifer,

I'm writing to you again—probably before you've even received my last letter—because I just realized that that letter was pretty much all about me, which was kind of rude. I didn't mean to ignore what you told me about Starla and Chris and Pat and the baby.

I'm dying to know more about Starla and Pat, but I really want to know why Chris is mean to you. Why does she tease you all the time? I HATE when people are mean to each other. (I guess I'm thinking about myself—and about the kids at my school, who aren't exactly being nice to Missy and Justin and me right now. Sorry this got turned back to me again.) Anyway, please supply details about Chris, and know that over here in Connecticut someone is on your side.

As for the baby, I'm torn between thinking how much fun a baby will be and imagining how difficult this is going to be for Pat and the rest of your family. I think babies are fun, don't you? But they're the most fun when they aren't actually yours. I would like to have a baby for about three hours. That would be ideal. What is Pat going to do after the baby is born? Will she be able to stay in school? I hope you're not somehow going to get stuck baby-sitting all the time. I'm feeling a little nervous since you wrote that your summer job was baby-sitting. Do not, I repeat, do NOT let your family make you do that.

I just reread what I wrote and I hope I'm not being pushy again. But I'm worried that since you're the youngest in your family, maybe the others think they can boss you around?????

Now as for Starla, she really does seem very cool. And even though she dropped out of school, it sounds like she's a good influence on you. But I'm wondering . . . why is she your SECRET best friend????? And who are you keeping her a secret from?

I'd better sign off. Mom wants us to have a family conference in about five minutes. It was pitifully easy to arrange a family conference since Mom and Dad are both home all day now. And here is the lovely subject of the conference: How to stretch our remaining dollars as far as possible. Mom is probably going to make up one of the giant charts she's famous for. I mean, famous in our family. By the end of the meeting it will be full of reminders such as: If you can use it again, don't throw it out!!! (Mom's reminders always end with multiple !'s.)

Please write when you can and fill me in on your life. I need to concentrate on someone else's life in order to keep my mind off my own.

Love,
Allie

November 11
Dear Allie,

I got both of your letters—the second one just came today—and I was really happy to have them. However . . . I was <u>SO</u> sorry to hear about your parents and their jobs. I can't believe it—any of it. I mean, it must have been hard enough when your dad's job got "eliminated" (yeah—stupid term), but then to find out that you'll have to go to a new school in the middle of the year, and on top of that, for your mom to lose her job too? Allie, I'm not even sure what to say, except that I'm here. That sounds really lame, but you know what I mean (I hope). I feel like your friend, even though we haven't met. Each time I get one of your letters and see your thoughts and words in your own handwriting, it's almost as good as a visit. I want you to know I think of you a lot, if that helps at all right now.

Okay, so I'm going to try to take your mind off things by answering your questions. Oh, wait! I almost forgot—your school picture! Thank you for sending it. I love your curly, curly hair. It makes me want to start a collection of photos of <u>excellent</u> hairdos. You are so lucky to have hair like that. Also, I can tell from your photo (as if I didn't already know from your letters) that you are one of those people who are just truly NICE. You've said you think you're pushy, and maybe you are a little, well, let's just say assertive. And overly ambitious. But you do things from your heart.

Now back to your questions. Regarding my hair: it

doesn't reach my waist, but it does go about halfway down my back. Starla likes that because she says it has lots more styling possibilities than short hair. (Starla plans on attending cosmetology school.) Sometimes when I've been to Starla's apartment after she's finished her shift at the Coffee Cup and she's done something new with my hair, I have to brush it out on my way home. Otherwise my father will get suspicious. (I've never confessed this to Starla.)

Which brings me to two more of your questions: Why is Starla a secret, and who's she a secret from? The answer to the first question is: She's a secret because Dad disapproves of her. He's met her at the Coffee Cup a few times and he knows we're friendly, but he thinks she's wasting her life, and also that she's a bad influence on me because of walking away from her family and dropping out and wanting to go to cosmetology school instead of regular college. And, all right, she has about a dozen piercings. Even I can't look at some of them without cringing (on the inside). But I don't understand why my father can't accept the good things about Starla. For instance, it must take a lot of courage to leave a bad situation behind when you're still only sixteen and find a way to support yourself and even plan on furthering your education, don't you think? And considering how mean Chris is to me—not to mention that Pat is about to become an unwed teenage mother—Starla seems like a better influence than either of them.

As for the other question about Starla, she's mainly a secret from Dad, like I said. He thinks it's bad enough that we talk at the Coffee Cup. I could never let him know that I go over to her apartment all the time. And since Dad sometimes stops in at the Coffee Cup for coffee (duh, what else?), a bunch of the workers know him, know me, know Starla. So I have to be very careful about visiting her. I'm afraid Dad's going to find out someday. He'd be furious— and I wouldn't even have done anything wrong!

To change the subject: What's going to happen after Pat has her baby? I don't know exactly, but believe me, it will NOT involve my taking care of the baby. That's Pat's job. My grandparents have made that very clear.

As for Chris and why she's mean to me, the answer is: I'm not sure. She doesn't like me. That _is_ for sure. But I don't really know why. She's jealous and she tries to sabotage me so that she can look better than me, or at least so that I won't look so good. And I know she hates it when I win awards. Also, I'm the youngest, so maybe she thinks she can pick on me. I guess I'm an easy target because I don't fight back.

You know why I don't fight back? I tell myself it's because it isn't worth it, that one day I'm going to be out of here. I'll get to college (somehow) and find a job and never look back. But the truth is, I'm a little afraid of Chris. Which is why I can understand what Starla did. I understand about needing to leave.

Sorry to sound so negative. Anyway, can you see why I like the peace of Starla's apartment, where nobody criticizes me and (more important) somebody thinks I'm wonderful and believes in me?

Okay. It's really late. I'm writing this by flashlight in bed and Ava is telling me that the light is keeping her up, which is a lie, but I'd better stop here.

Love,

Jennifer

P.S. I'm enclosing two examples from my bad hairdo photo collection. You can keep them.

~~~~~~~~~~~~~~~~~~~

November 15

Dear Jennifer,

1. I think you're wonderful.
2. I believe in you.
3. I'm glad we're friends.

Love,

Allie

~~~~~~~~~~~~~~~~~~~

November 19

Dear Allie,

Thank you. I saved the note with your letters in a tin box under my bed. I've taken the note out and reread it twice so far—once when Chris called me Pinocchio and once when she laughed at a poem I'd written (which she found by snooping in my private stuff). Maybe the next poem I write will be about a pig named Chris. Ha, ha.

Love,

Jennifer

November 22, Thanksgiving
Dear Jennifer,

I have so many things to say that I don't know where to begin. First of all, as you know, I've been saving your letters too. Yesterday I made a folder for them and I got out my scrapbooking stuff and decorated the folder with ribbons and stickers. I glued your school picture in the center and stamped FRIENDSHIP under it.

One of the many good things about your letters is that I can take them with me wherever I go . . . which is important, since my parents have decided that we're going to move to Rhode Island. Right after Christmas. You'll be coming with me, but I'll have to leave my other friends behind.

I can't believe it. I'm so sad that now I don't think I can finish this letter after all. I guess I'll have to tell you the rest of the story later.

Love,
Allie

November 22
Dear Allie,

Happy Thanksgiving! You know how most people celebrate the holiday with turkey and stuffing and gravy, the family all seated around a big table? Guess how we celebrated today. Eating cheese sandwiches in a hospital waiting room while Pat had her baby. Yup, it finally happened. Savion Isaiah arrived this morning. He only weighed six pounds and he needed oxygen at first and I'm sorry to have to report this, but he is UG-LEE. He's doing okay now, though, and so is Pat, but believe me, you've never heard so much shrieking. The nurse would say, "Push!" and Pat would go, "AUGHHHHHHHH!!!!!!!!" like in a horror movie. There was sort of a lot of blood too. I don't think I'll ever get pregnant myself, not in a million years. But Pat looked down at that ugly squirming thing in her lap and said she was in love with it. Savion's father, Brandon, doesn't seem quite as enthusiastic. He left us all at the hospital about an hour after Savion was born, roaring off on his ridiculous motorcycle, and making me gladder than ever that I have set aside Pat's $$ for diapers, etc. I'll give it back to her a week or so after she and Savion come home from the hospital and the expenses start piling up. I don't think Pat will be tempted to give any of it to Brandon by then.

So, can you believe it? I have a new cousin. A cousin once removed, I guess, even though Savion feels more like a nephew. I have one or two nights left in the bottom bunk and then I'll switch to the cot. And Squally Redface will take up residence in the next room with Pat.

How was your Thanksgiving?

Love,

Jennifer

November 23
Dear Jennifer,

I guess I'll try to finish yesterday's letter. I'm so upset that I can hardly concentrate on anything. Anyway, here's what happened: Mom and Dad and Missy and Justin and I had just sat down to Thanksgiving dinner—only the five of us this year, no relatives or neighbors or "stray" friends (Dad's term) because that would have been too expensive—and we had said grace over the food, which included the puniest turkey I've ever seen, when Mom, looking all bright and cheery, stood up and said, "I have an announcement to make."

Now, given what's been going on in our family, and also the fact that she was grinning away, wouldn't you have expected her to say that she or Dad had gotten a job? Especially since she had waited until a festive family gathering to make the announcement? Well, I did. So you can imagine my surprise when she said, "We're moving to Rhode Island."

There was a clunk then as Missy, Justin, and I all dropped our forks at the same time. (Justin's fell on the floor and Beauty scarfed up the piece of turkey that had been attached to it.)

"What?" shrieked Missy, and then she began to cry, which is what I wanted to do, but since I'm the oldest I thought I should set an example of bravery for my sister and brother.

Well, anyway, the short version of this story is that

Mom and Dad don't have any job leads and they can't afford the rent on our house if they aren't working, so we're going to R.I. to live with Mom's parents. That way, Mom and Dad can take their time finding work because they won't have to worry about paying bills for a while. They had paid our rent through December 31st, though, so we'll have one more Christmas in our house and then we'll move.

Jennifer, I'm just so upset. I've never lived anywhere but here. I don't want to leave all my friends behind. I don't know anyone in R.I. except Granny and Grandpa. It was bad enough having to switch schools, but moving AWAY? Plus, Missy and I will probably wind up sharing a room with Justin—a SECOND-GRADER. How am I going to get through this?

Love,
Allie

~~~~~~

November 26
Dear Allie,

You'll get through it. Partly because you have to, and partly because I think you're the kind of person who'll make friends pretty easily. I know you don't want to leave Lucinda and move into a house that will be crowded, but you do what you have to do. Take it from someone who knows. Pat and Savion the Howler, aka Squally Redface, are home and Chris has set up camp with Ava and me, and

I am TRYING to find some peace and privacy, but I mostly only find it at Starla's place.

By the way, last night Pat was moaning about the cost of diapers (what a surprise) and I handed her the envelope with her $$ in it and she said, "Where did this come from?" and I was like, "I just found it. Under the couch." She squinted at me because she didn't believe me, but when she counted the $$ and found every penny there, she could hardly accuse me of stealing it. So now the $$ will be put to good use.

But back to you, Allie. I'm really sorry about what's happening. I know you wish everything in your life could stay the same—I mean, the same as it was a few months ago. Here's one thing that won't change: me. We can be pen pals wherever we live, and have our "letter visits" forever—until we're little old ladies. Okay?

Lots of Love,
Jennifer

~~~~~~~~~~~~~~~~~~~~~~~~~~~~~~

December 1
Dear Jennifer,

Thank you for your letter. Guess what. You're the first person I told my news to. I didn't even tell Lucinda until two days after Thanksgiving. (She cried, by the way, which made me cry, and then we couldn't eat the popcorn we'd just made.) I felt better after reading your letter. I really appreciate all the things you said. And yes, I hope

we're pen pals forever—unless one day we actually meet
and then we settle down in the same town and become
next-door neighbors and can be regular pals instead of
pen pals.

So Squally Redface has arrived! I laughed out loud
when I read that name. But I feel so bad that you feel
out of place in your own home. That isn't fair. By the
way, I want you to know that I may complain, and I may be
afraid about moving, not to mention sharing a room with
Justin in addition to Missy, but mostly I know how lucky I
am. You're right. I do wish nothing had to change. Still, I'm
really grateful for my family and you and my other friends
and my brother and sister and cat and dogs and ferret
and grandparents. I know everything will be okay
eventually.

> XXXOOO
> Allie

~~~~~~~~~~~~~~~~~~~~~~~~~~~~~

December 8
Dear Jennifer,

Is everything all right? I have a feeling maybe things
aren't so good at your house. Please write when you have
a chance. I miss hearing from you.

> Love,
> Allie

~~~~~~~~~~~~~~~~~~~~~~~~~~~~~

December 11
Dear Allie,

Starla is gone. I don't know what to do.
Love,
Jennifer

~~~~~~~~~~~~~~~~~~~~~~~~~~~~~~~

December 12
Dear Allie,

Sorry I sent that letter yesterday. I guess I felt like you did when you found out you were moving. I just can't believe Starla's gone, but she is. And now I have no one to escape to and no place to escape to. But much worse than that—I don't even know if Starla's okay.

This is what happened: I hadn't seen Starla in a few days, so finally I got up the nerve to ask the manager of the Coffee Cup if she knew where she was, and she said she hadn't been showing up for work, and in fact, if I found her to tell her she was fired. (Yeah, right.) So I went to her apartment and she didn't answer the bell. I sat in the hall and waited for an hour until the super happened to come along. He said Starla had packed up and moved out a couple of days earlier. He didn't know why. And he didn't know where she had gone. And I have no idea how to look for her. She didn't leave a forwarding address, and she doesn't have a cell phone, and anyway, I have this feeling that maybe she doesn't want to be found. But what do you think could have happened? I hope wherever she is she found a good job. And nice people. And that her dream of going to cosmetology school will come true. I hope she left for a good reason, and I hope she's all right. But I wish she had said good-bye.

Love,
Jennifer

~~~~~~~~~~~~~~

December 15
Dear Jennifer,

Oh, no. I'm so sorry. I can't believe your letter.

Listen, you have to promise me something. Promise me that you'll find—somewhere—the peace and privacy you used to find at Starla's. You need that.

How can I help you?

Love,
Allie

P.S. I know Starla was your best friend, but remember that I'm your friend too.

~~~~~~~~~~~~~~

December 18
Dear Allie,
Thanks. And Merry Christmas. You've been a very good friend.

Love,
Jennifer

~~~~~~~~~~~~~~~~~~

December 21
Dear Jennifer,

You sounded kind of like you were saying good—bye in
your last letter. Were you? Please don't stop writing. You
can't stop now. I mean, we can't. We're forever friends.
And our stories aren't over. Please, please, please, please
write back. But in case I don't hear from you for a while,
Merry Christmas to you too.

Oh, and from now on you'll have to send your letters
to me at home, not through Mr. Jessop, obviously. I'm going
to write my new address on a card that you can keep in
your purse or your notebook or someplace safe—maybe
with your bad hairdo photo collection. Don't lose it!

And PLEASE WRITE BACK.

Love,
Allie

~~~~~~~~~~~~~~~~~~

December 24
Dear Allie,

You won't believe what's been happening! I can't even
believe it. Actually, two things have happened, both good.
Now, before you get your hopes up . . . No, Starla is not
back, and I haven't heard from her.

Anyway—well, I know this is really silly, but because I've been feeling desperate, a few days ago I made a wish on a star. At least I think it was a star. It could have been a very slow-moving plane, but whatever it was, I wished on it. And due to my desperation, I made <u>three</u> wishes. I wished that Starla would show up, I wished that Dad would sell an invention, and I wished that my grandmother would finally win the lottery, since she's been buying tickets since before I was born. I don't know how stars (or planes) work, but two of my wishes did not come true, one did, and something really great that I hadn't dared to wish for has also happened. I suppose I could make you guess about the wishes, like I did with Pat and Chris, but I'm not going to do that. Here's the wish breakdown:

1. Starla did not show up. (You already knew that.)

2. Dad did not sell an invention.

3. But my grandmother did win the lottery!!!!!! All right, she only won $325, and over the years she must have spent thousands of bucks on tickets, but believe me, we can use $325 right before Christmas, so that wish came true!

Now for the wish that I <u>didn't</u> make on the star/plane that came true anyway. Are you ready? Hold on to your hat, as my dad would say. . . . On the last day of school before vacation, Ms. Dennis asked me to see her during lunch period. When I went to her office, she looked all serious and she told me to take a seat. I was starting to get nervous, but guess what she said. She said, "Jennifer, you are hands-down my best student this year, and one of the top students in the school. Have you given any thought to next year?" She meant was I going to apply to any of the special high schools in Castleton. They're public schools, but you have to do all sorts of things to get into them, and I hadn't dared to ask my father for help. He's no good at that sort of thing, and it would have made him anxious. I had just assumed I'd go to the local high school (think metal detectors, broken windows, library closed due to water damage, etc.) and work as hard as I could.

But Ms. Dennis says she knows I can get into any high school I want, and she's going to help me! She's going to find out when the tests are, and get applications for me, and even drive me to interviews. Isn't that amazing? This really is my dream come true.

I'm so happy that I don't care about Squally Redface (he has the healthiest set of lungs in Castleton) or having Chris crammed into our bedroom or . . . well, I was about to add "Starla," but that wouldn't have been true. I do care about Starla. And I miss her. But I'm trying to focus on Ms. Dennis's news, and Christmas.

Sorry this letter was once again all about me. That doesn't mean I haven't been thinking about you. Please let me know how your Christmas is. And how the move goes. I guess the next letter you write will be from your grandparents' house. Tell me all the news! I can't wait to hear it.

Lots of Love,

Your Forever Friend, Jennifer

~~~~~~~~~~~~~~~~~~~~~~~~~~~~~~

January 18
Dear Jennifer,

I hate it here.

> Love,
> Allie

~~~~~~~~~~~~~~~~~~~~~~~~~~~~~~

January 23
Dear Allie,

Now that is not a proper letter. Mr. Jessop would be appalled. You know I need more news than that. I'm sorry things are bad. (You have to tell me why, exactly, you hate Rhode Island.) But remember that things are never going to be <u>all</u> good. For instance, I've been on two school interviews (very good), but I still have to face Chris every day and we're all being awakened all night long by Squally Redface. And Starla is not back. But I'm so excited about school next year that that's really the only thing I can think about.

So come on. In your next letter I dare you to tell me three things you're grateful for.

Love,
Jennifer
P.S. Remember when I told you that I used to wish for a best friend, and then I met Starla? Well, Starla may be gone, but I know I can always visit with you.

February 2
Dear Jennifer,

Happy Groundhog Day!

Okay, you're right. Things are never going to be all good. But thanks to your dare, I can list more than three things I'm grateful for. Here goes:

1. I'm grateful that I'm not in my old school where the kids (except for Lucinda) were treating Missy and Justin and me like something disgusting you'd want to avoid on the sidewalk.

2. I'm grateful to have a fresh start. (I guess that's actually part of #1.)

3. I'm grateful to my grandparents for letting us move in with them.

4. I'm grateful that the groundhog did not see his shadow this morning, which for some weird reason means that spring is on the way.

5. And, thinking over what you said in your last letter, I'm grateful to Mr. Jessop because if he hadn't come up with his pen pal assignment, you and I wouldn't be friends. (I almost can't imagine that, can you?)

A couple of months ago you said you knew I wished everything could stay the same, but guess what? I don't wish that anymore. I miss our house and living in the country, but there are a lot of things I don't miss, and even better, there are a lot of things I'm looking forward to. Not long after I told you I hate it here, my new homeroom teacher announced that we're going to spend this semester raising money for a weekend trip to a beach in Connecticut where we'll do a project on ecology. (Yippee! Collecting money! My favorite thing.) Also, there's this really cute boy in my math class. His name is Sean and, well, I'll keep you posted. I think he's noticed me.

So . . . I'm glad my wish didn't come true. And I'm glad some of yours did. I can't wait to hear how our stories are going to turn out.

Lots of Love,
Your Pen Pal, Allie

P.S. I don't know if you remember the poem you sent me. Do you? I hope you keep copies of everything you write, and put all your poems and stories someplace safe. Anyway, in case you don't remember, this is the poem:

"Good—bye," he said
and strode away
clapping his hat
on his head.
And I called after him,
"You'll be back. I know you."
But his footfall
faded.
Maybe this isn't a bad thing.
There will be others
who will come along
with a surer step.

Two things, Jennifer:

1. I just want you to know that I read this over and over again. Partly because you wrote it and partly because I think it has a really hopeful message. Did you mean it to be hopeful? (It's funny that you wrote it before Starla left.)

2. It doesn't have a title, so I'm going to give it one. I know—pushy, pushy. But I don't care. Your poem is important and it deserves a title. So it is now called "What's Around the Corner." I think it (the poem, I mean, not the title) applies to lots of things in our lives that we're afraid of but that have happy endings.

P.P.S. Write back soon!

Love Again,
Allie

Refugee receiving a grain allowance from World Food Programme supplies.
Photo Credit: *UNHCR / H. Caux*

NAOMI SHIHAB NYE

SECRET SONG

Wishing is an open bowl.
I used to have one of my own.
It was shiny inside, with a wide fresh mouth.

I saw the bowl recently
in someone else's hands.
Till now I am hoping

a person would say to me—
Please, could you help me hold this bowl?
And I would be so happy to.

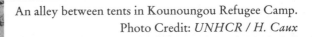
An alley between tents in Kounoungou Refugee Camp.
Photo Credit: *UNHCR / H. Caux*

CYNTHIA VOIGT

THE STEPSISTER

The Stepfather weighed over nineteen stone, broad as a bear in his embroidered velveteen waistcoat. He was clumsy around them, loud-voiced, as if he were bellowing about in his warehouses. They forbade him entry to their salon. This freshly painted room was furnished with the choicest pieces from their former, grander home, the dainty-legged chairs and tables, gilt mirrors, carved German cupboards displaying Venetian glassware and Chinese porcelains. The Stepfather traded in teas and coffees, spices, perfumes, so he had promised to tell his captains to keep a lookout for the best pieces of Venetian glassware and Chinese porcelains, and to spare no expense. The Mother shook her head, gently but firmly, to tell him: No, my dear, you are men, how could you be expected to have a dainty eye, you will end up foolishly wasting money if you attempt this gift. He almost— As the Mother guided him out of the salon, his thick arm almost struck a shelf of glasses so small, they might hold only three thimblefuls of liquor, blue, with rims of white glass spun like lace.

Which would have been a tragic loss, if the Mother had not kept him from it.

Yetiffe, who was the youngest and burdened with more imagination than the others, thought of them as a triptych. Not a holy triptych, for that would be a vainglorious thought, but a secular one. The Mother, with her fine eyes and high proud forehead, stood full length in the center portrait, with Lysette's head in profile on one side of her and Yetiffe's head in profile on the other. The tone of each portrait was the same, the colors bathed in light; the clever gray eyes were the same in each of the three faces. They were a mother and her two daughters. They were two sisters and their mother. They turned to one another, like a triptych closing.

They had a salon when the Mother married the widower; they had a carriage. They had each her own bedchamber, on the first floor, Yetiffe's and Lysette's rooms at a distance from their mother's, as they had been before their own father died and the great house they had lived in gone to his brother, who had sired sons to inherit the estate. The house the Stepfather moved them into didn't entirely lack grandeur, and they were grateful. Although they had hoped for personal maids and there was only the stepsister, a pretty enough girl, but she lacked their strength of character. And even if the house had no great staircase, had neither ballroom nor stables, nor majordomo nor more than a cook who lived out and the two little maids for the heavy cleaning and washing, still they could remember to be grateful.

As could the Stepfather, for the honor their mother did in marrying him and allowing him to stand as father to her two daughters. He could, and he did, remember how much he had to thank the well-born widow for. For example, his house would never have opened its door to one of the King's footmen, who presented a paper sealed with the King's royal signet, had he had not married their mother. Yetiffe took the folded paper from the stepsister—who had answered the knock on the door, looking for all anyone would know like one of the servants of the house. Which was a blessing, because her manner was too modest for a daughter of such a house as this had become, when the Stepfather brought them to it. If she had been a genuine domestic servant she couldn't have done better. Yetiffe read the words of address: The Merchant Orlov and His Family.

So they could open the message without delay, and know that they were invited—at the Queen's pleasure, at the King's behest—to a ball.

A great ball, the word spread quickly, the grandest of balls, to which were summoned all the maidens of the country so that they might all be presented to the King's son, who was of an age to wed, and of a mind.

Yetiffe would wear rosy pink, which color brought out the pink tones of her pale skin. She must have her garnet coronet to set off her dark hair, and red roses to cascade down her skirts. The satin dancing slippers for her feet, which were as fine-boned as her hands, must be dyed to match the garnets.

Luckily, the stepsister dressed hair, whether plain for every day or elegant for evening, as well as any real lady's maid could.

Luckily, she was a clever seamstress, so Yetiffe could hope to have fresh roses at her slender waist on the night of the ball. Lysette would wear yellow, for her skin was browner, and scattered with freckles. Lysette would have no flowers, would wear instead amber, at her neck and in her coronet. "You must do something original with amber on my hem and sleeves," Lysette told the stepsister, because Lysette was sturdier that Yetiffe, her waist, like her hands and feet, less small and dainty and in need of disguise and distraction.

Luckily, the stepsister slept little, so they didn't have to fret about having their gowns ready on time. "It's too bad you can't come with us," they said to her. "We'll bring you sweets—if we have a chance to carry some away with us. We'll tell you everything that happens, and how it is to dance with the Prince. If he dances a waltz with bold turns, how he holds his partner's waist. I'm sorry," they said when they saw how dejected the girl grew.

"What would you wear, if you were going to the ball?" Yetiffe asked, to cheer her.

"A gown of white," she answered, so readily that they knew she had dreamed of going. White was a good color for her creamy skin, they agreed. "White as sea foam. And pearls in my hair." This they agreed showed some taste and a realistic sense of what it was possible to wear if your hair was as gold as the coins of the realm. "But no other jewels."

"Bare-necked?" Lysette asked, and said, "It's lucky you aren't going, if that is how you would present yourself. To the Prince. Before the world. Did you make a sweet custard for today's dinner? Did you polish the silver bowls, and the silver platters, and the silver forks, spoons, knives?"

Yes and yes, the stepsister answered, but why should she sound impatient at the question? Did she not care for the honor of the house?

"For I am very hungry," Lysette said.

"And our father's cousin is bringing her two sons to dine with us today," Yetiffe said.

"Everyone looks forward to the sweet at the end of the meal, but especially young gentlemen."

"It's too bad that you'll be so fully occupied in the kitchen that you must miss the dinner, and the two sons."

"We are always so jolly together."

"But you can see them when you serve. And we'll tell you all that we say among ourselves, the jests especially."

"Except you must not ask us to remember all the jests, when we are so very merry."

"And you must tell us which of the gentlemen you judge the better choice for husband."

The stepsister's blue eyes filmed with tears, and she bit her lip with vexation, to miss all the gaiety. She tried to hide this, as if she needed to cough, but Yetiffe understood her. However, for the evening to pass pleasurably, as it should at her mother's table, the stepsister must be too busy to have a chance to sit down to dinner with the company. "What will I wear?" Lysette asked Yetiffe, who answered, "I shall wear my blue silk gown, and my sapphires."

The Stepfather hired a coach and six to carry them all to the palace doors on the great night of the ball. It was a windy, mysterious, and black night. The stepsister held the carriage door open for them, bracing it against the wind. Her face glowed pale in the moonlight whenever the moon could break free from behind the clouds, to shine light down. In the coach they sat two to each side, facing each other, all four transfixed by anxiety, and excitement, and their own dreams. The Stepfather crowded his corner of the carriage, and his waistcoat gleamed as white as the moon. At the palace door, he waited while the King's footman handed down the three women, and then he emerged from the carriage. He accompanied his new wife up the stairs and into the palace from which—had he not been married to her—he would have been barred. The common people, who had nothing better to do, cheered from the roadside, or made mock from the darkness beneath the trees where the torchlight didn't reach. The Stepfather stayed at their side until their names were announced to the splendid gathering and they could descend into the ballroom. There he left them, to join the other fathers at the card tables.

The Mother found a chair for herself at the thronged edges of the room and set her two daughters out before her on smaller chairs. They waited for their dance cards to fill up. Yetiffe, the youngest, waited in rosy pink; Lysette waited in buttery yellow, her skirt scattered with glowing amber stones.

"Wouldn't our stepsister wish to be here now," they said.

They said this at every new wonder—the forty violins, the handsome cavalry captain, the Prince and Queen and King making their entrance in a blinding wave of royalty, the duchess's diamonds. "We must tell her of this," they said. They opined that there would be dishes she would wish she could taste when the midnight buffet would be served; perhaps she could duplicate them for their own table. They knew how she would have liked to dance with the Prince, as they did, first Lysette, who was the older. He danced with each unmarried woman in the room.

Each unmarried woman of eligible age, that is, for matrimony was the purpose of this ball. All understood this, although none spoke of it. The captains of cavalry and sons of ministers, the lords from their country estates and all of their male cousins, they were present to assure each maiden a satisfying ball, partners in plenty; but not one of the gentlemen would have presumed to court a bride for himself. Not until the Prince had made his choice.

The Prince's choice was the great surprise of the evening. She surprised even the Prince, it seemed, arriving unfashionably late, just as the clocks struck ten, and standing unannounced at the center of the doorway, unaccompanied by any parent or duenna. A mask made of green apple leaves covered her face. The Prince rushed to her.

He danced with no one else after she had appeared. For waltz after flowing waltz that same couple danced together, he tall and straight as a birch tree, while her skirts billowed out, the color of waves when the moon shines out from behind clouds and silvers their foamy crests.

When the music ceased, the Prince escorted his masked lady all around the ballroom and introduced the daughters and their families. She smiled at everyone and held out her gloved hand to be bent over by the men. When the couple came over to Yetiffe and Lysette, and their mother, the lady repeated their names, and complimented them on their fine dress, and asked how they enjoyed the ball. She picked them out from the hundred and more in the ballroom to speak to; she sought them out to admire. She was a great lady and most likely a great beauty too, although, as the Mother pointed out, she was so soft-spoken she couldn't but lack strength of character. Yetiffe thought she might disagree with her mother about that, since the lady had shown them such attentions. How the stepsister would sigh, to hear of it; how all the others in the room now looked at them with admiration, and envy. How many questions were then asked of them, too. Who is she? What is her name? What is her family? Where is her home? To all of their eager partners Yetiffe and Lysette would say only that they could not answer those questions. All they could say was that she was a great and lovely lady, was she not?

At the midnight supper the questions came faster. Plates of dainty foods were brought to them where they sat, and goblets of wine. Where had she gone, this lady? Had she disappeared forever? Why had she left the ball so early, so precipitously? Would she return?

The Prince also came to ask, but they must say to him as to all the other lords and ladies that they could tell him nothing. "Why did she linger to talk with you, then?" the Prince asked.

"We can't tell you that," they said again. Yetiffe too was puzzled by the lady's notice. If it had been she whom the Prince had chosen to pay such attentions to, she would not have wanted to share the glory with anyone. Lysette remarked, as the Prince walked sadly away, "It must be that she could see by looking the kind of people we are. Not like these others."

"He will come back to you," their mother promised, arranging her heavy skirts. "He must, because we are his only link to her, and he'll hope to learn something from us. Even though we tell him nothing, he'll come back, because our nothing is worth more than the nothing everybody else knows."

She was proved prophetic. Lysette and Yetiffe had a successful ball, and as they were driven home at dawn, they could anticipate—sleepily, yawning, their toes now pinched by their dancing shoes—everything they had to tell the stepsister, who had missed all the wonders of the night. "How she will envy us," they said.

"How she will wish she had been with us, to take part in the lady's attentions."

"How she must long to be a real sister to us, Yetiffe."

"Yes, Lysette, and we must remember to be particularly kind and tell her everything that happened."

"All we saw."

"And heard."

"Ate and drank."

By next evening, stories had spread throughout the city and countryside. She was no lady, but a great princess, no, a queen, no, an immortal denizen of the land of fairies who had glimpsed the Prince and lost her heart to him. She would sacrifice all, leave all her familiar life and give up her immortality, too, to be with him. She was a magician's daughter, sent to steal the Prince's soul. She was a bold actress off the streets, hoping to hook the Prince by her beauty and reel him into marriage and thus with one bold cast to alter her state from actress to princess. She was a humble serving girl magicked by her fairy godmother—her dress magic, her coach and eight and serving men, too, magic—until the clock struck twelve. She was a maiden cleverer than most, who had found the very way to catch the Prince's eye and bring him to marriage.

Each time the Mother and her daughters went out, they heard a new story, which they brought home to talk over among themselves, if there were no ladies come to drink cups of chocolate offered to them from a heavy silver tray by the stepsister. They would talk, and weigh the information, and make judgment on each story. Then, when the story had grown dry and tired, they would take it down to the kitchen, where the stepsister's interest made it lively again, and they could savor it again, until they went out again to gather up the next story, or a visitor brought a new tale to them.

Rumor flourished, but the Prince languished. He slept badly and found no pleasure in even the daintiest foods. He read verses, and sometimes even wrote them. He sent messengers in all directions to find her.

He didn't even know her name.

Because she was masked, he couldn't even describe her face.

"Her voice is like music, like moonlight. When you hear her speak, you will know her voice," he told the messengers.

A week of this and the Kingdom was in an uproar. The King determined to give a second ball, three weeks hence. Invitations were hastily sent out.

Lysette wanted a gown as green as emeralds, with lace at the wrists and bodice; Yetiffe wanted a gown of silk as deep a blue as the evening sky before night has settled upon it, but she was the younger, so she had to wait longer for the stepsister to finish it and fit it. No other maiden would have gowns as wonderful as theirs, and all would once again ask Yetiffe and ask Lysette who their seamstress was.

It was the very afternoon of the ball when Yetiffe's dress was completed, and that left them with barely enough time for the stepsister to wash their hair, and brush it dry before the fire, and wind ribbons into the heavy dark strands she lifted and twisted and coiled. As the coach drove away, they could see her in the garden, where, in twilight, she was gathering in laundered sheets. A wind filled the sheets, blew them out into swellings and flowings like sea foam riding the waves into shore. They waved to her, but she did not see them.

It was the same ball, held again. In his red tunic and black trousers, the handsome Prince danced one dance with each maiden. Yetiffe could not have sworn to it, but she thought that the few words she and the Prince exchanged were also the same as before, something about the pleasantness of the music, something about the excitement of the ball. "This is a happy night," the Prince announced, his face turned away from his partner and toward the top of the wide staircase.

When the clock struck only nine, and there were maidens yet to be escorted through a dance by the Prince, the lady was standing in the doorway. She wore the same dress as before. It billowed out like sheets on a line. Her cloud-colored mask was made of the silvery leaves of birches, and the Prince crossed the wide dance floor to take her hand and lead her out among the dancers, and dance with no other as the night went on.

Once again, the lady visited the chairs where Lysette and Yetiffe sat, their mother silent behind them. Of the young couple, it was the lady alone who spoke, for the Prince had no intention of taking his eyes from her even for a moment. She complimented them for the elegance of their dress and asked after the pleasures of their evening. They said, "Thank you, my lady," and "Yes, my lady." The lady did not like to be long out of the arms of her Prince, so she didn't linger in conversation, and they were none the wiser about her, for all of the attentions she had paid them.

Others, however, didn't know this. Lysette's dance card filled with partners, as did Yetiffe's. They sat down to the midnight supper within a circle of admirers, all beseeching them to tell what they knew of the lady, all bemoaning the sisters' discreet tongues. Yetiffe and Lysette were too busy and happy to attend to anything else, so it was news of their own conquests they carried home to the stepsister, who waited up for them with hot mulled wine and carried away their worn dancing slippers. It was she who told them, the next day, about the lady.

The stepsister brought news back from the market. The hog butcher had told her how the lady had once again disappeared, long before dawn ended the ball, the greengrocer thought before supper was served; this was what his wife had heard. The baker predicted that the Prince would not wait more than two weeks for another ball. The milkman's sister's sister-in-law worked in the palace kitchen and he reported that the King and Queen were almost as distraught as their son, fearing as they did that the lady might be the Queen of the Fairies, the old stories brought to life, and their son might already be lost to them forever.

"Two weeks! How will my gown ever be ready in that time? Will our stepfather forbid us new dresses? How would it be if I wore a golden gown?" Lysette asked. "I am the older," she said.

"Mine will be silver as moonlight," Yetiffe answered. "The skirt sewn with pearls, like dew in moonlight."

But the Stepfather refused to buy the pearls. "Fabric—and fine fabrics, lace also—and another set of dancing slippers," he said, "those you may have. But no more jewels. You'll bankrupt me," he said, from where he filled the doorway to the salon. So the stepsister sewed tiny white pebbles into the skirt instead. Where she found them, Yetiffe didn't know.

"You are so clever," Yetiffe told the stepsister. "I never want to be parted from you, you are so clever. And pretty, too," she added. "Although there are those who say your face lacks character." Yetiffe had never had so heavy a skirt. All would wish to have a gown like hers, once they had seen her. It was almost a queen's skirt she wore.

Not that Yetiffe dreamed that the Prince loved her. But a prince could not always choose to wed the she he loved, even though whoever a prince wed would be the queen.

They drove off to the ball on a warm evening, just as the sun was slipping behind the clouds at earth's end. The gentle golden light shone on the white feathery bellies of the doves that rose up in alarm in the courtyard, so loud did the horses' hooves clatter. The doves rose up in a wave around the carriage, like sea foam stirred by the wind.

The mysterious lady came on time to that ball, which itself opened impatiently early. Her mask was made of the petals of white roses, their edges tinged with a pale pink. She wore the same gown she had worn twice before, as white as the soft bellies of doves.

This time she spoke only with the Prince and he only with her. They stood and talked more than they danced, he tall and strong, she slender and graceful. They laughed, for all to see, and leaned toward each other. They were watched by all.

Not all who watched watched in envy. Some watched in worry. The guards and ministers were never all that far from the young couple, nor did the King and Queen relax their vigilance. All of the guests, too, watched closely, for the third is the well-known charm, and the fairies, especially, practice charms. But these guards did not keep the Prince close, for two reasons. The first was that he would not tolerate it; so that, for example, when the Prince and the masked lady stepped outside to walk along the balustrade, guards followed them to the opened French doors but remained within. The second reason for maintaining distance was this: The lady had, on the previous occasions, danced until the supper was being set out on the tables. In the first hours of the ball, then, she would remain at the Prince's side.

Except, of course, when she must be excused from the company, to do that which every living creature needs to do. The Prince bent his head to hear her request; that, Yetiffe could see. Yetiffe was near enough to see pink rise into the Prince's cheek at the lady's question and guess what it must be, before her partner whirled her away. To her chagrin, it was Lysette—partnerless for the gavotte and so able to watch events with her full attention—who could report what happened next. The Prince walked at the lady's side up the staircase, and at its top gestured with his arm to point her in the direction she should go, to reach the room she sought. He stood waiting. Now he was watching her when no one else could any longer see her.

Then he stiffened where he stood.

Then he ran off. If he called out, the music buried his voice as he ran. It took the guards a full minute to notice that he was gone, and themselves surge up the long flight of stairs after him.

The King and Queen had by that time risen from their thrones in alarm.

Abruptly, the music ceased.

The dancers froze in place.

Into an echoing silence the Prince returned, holding in his hand a dancing slipper of pure glass, his face as pale and lifeless as the shoe. At a signal from the King, the musicians struck up the sprightly piece again.

Yetiffe almost wished to leave the ball then, so she could see the stepsister's eyes widen at this new development. Except that the lady had not on this occasion singled them out and made them the envy of the room, she might have pleaded a headache and been taken home, where she could speak confidingly to her stepsister. "How I wish you had been there to actually be a part of the excitement. How you would have liked to have seen her, and how he looked at her, and how his heart was broken, as any fool could see in his face." But Yetiffe didn't leave the ball. There were captains and lieutenants in need of partners, and ministers' sons, and lords come in from the countryside for the occasion. There was news to hear and pass on, for soon everyone knew the Prince's plan.

He would send the glass slipper to every house. His lady

alone had feet small enough to fit into the glass slipper, and she alone was his chosen wife.

Yetiffe did not tell her thoughts then, not to anyone. The glass slipper was set out, for all to see, and she stared at it where it stood on its blue silk cushion, as if she wished later to draw it from memory. She held it in the palm of her hand. Only she and Lysette dared to handle the slipper so intimately; they were the only ones to whom the lady had spoken. Except for the Prince, of course.

The lady had, of course, spoken to the prince at great length.

But she had spoken to no other, unless you counted her curtsy and "Good evening, sir, good evening, madam," to the King and Queen. Yetiffe didn't count that. She made her plan.

To be princess, and later queen, was to be someone all must admire, and from whom all must welcome any attentions, however small. To be princess was to be picked out, set upon a high place while the people cheered from below. To be queen set you above sister, and mother too, and even aristocratic father were he still living, over even all men in the kingdom, excepting always the King.

Few would be your equal in the whole world.

That night Yetiffe did not sleep. She lay on her bed until all four stories of the Stepfather's house grew still. She listened for long minutes after the dark silence had settled into the house, moving slowly as a sun pulling light down into the western sky.

Was that the wind? making the shutters creak like a thief on the stairs. Was that a thief? knowing that whatever jewels a rich household possessed would be laid out in the mistress's chamber on the night of the ball. Yetiffe pulled the bedclothes up over her head, making a safe velvet darkness within the forbidding blackness of night.

Later—she did not think she had slept—there was what sounded like an owl's cry, or a rabbit's. Yetiffe crept out of bed then, and opened her window to a starry night. She slid the soft linen cover from her fat feather pillow and took out her scissors, to make long linen strips. She took a slim stick out of the wood box and wrapped one of the linen strips around it. She crept down the stairs to the starlit kitchen, where coals still burned hot in the fireplace, and as she hacked off her thick, bony heel, she bit down hard on the stick. Any sound might awaken the house and it was secrecy she counted on for the working out of her plan. The silence trembled all around her, but it did not shatter. It was not long before she could crawl back up the staircase—which creaked only once—and back up into her high bed, where she wrapped her foot in linen strips and feverishly awaited the day, and the Prince.

It was only messengers who came to the door, however, bearing a glass slipper. This looked to be the exact same dancing slipper they had seen the night before, so—when they had said yes, there were two unmarried daughters of the house—Yetiffe was shocked when Lysette's right foot slipped easily into the dainty shoe.

It was the right slipper that had been left behind.

"Ah," the messenger said. "Have you the mate?"

Lysette, pale, almost speechless, shook her head and whispered, "No. Shattered, smashed." To Yetiffe, Lysette seemed somehow altered, but Yetiffe herself felt icy hot, and weak as a woman after childbirth, not herself. And now this shocking thing, Lysette's foot fitting into the glass slipper that would be worn by the Prince's bride, who would be the Queen, and all would be her inferiors.

A sister, however, would be closer to the Queen than any other lady of the Kingdom, and so Yetiffe said not a word as Lysette rose to her feet, both of her hands clutching the messenger's arm.

Lysette's smile was proud, and she breathed in a hissing breath as she looked back at her sister and their mother, and the Stepfather. She walked awkwardly and Yetiffe thought she knew why. Lysette was no more the masked lady of the Prince's heart than she was.

In the doorway, Lysette stumbled, clutched at her escort's arm, took two steps, tottered onto the sidewalk, and fell down in a faint. Everyone gasped, rushed near, carried her inside, called for water, called for a doctor, said no doctor was necessary, it was only exhaustion from the ball and excitement of this event. The stepsister held a crystal bowl of cool water to Lysette's lips while their mother held Lysette's head elevated against her shoulder.

Lysette moaned.

So Yetiffe knelt down and pulled off the glass slipper. She pulled the lacy stocking down her sister's right leg and down over her sister's right foot. This revealed five stumps, one broader than the others and one as tiny as a baby's knuckle. The stumps were as black as those wounds a surgeon has cauterized, and they oozed black blood.

Yetiffe pushed her own right foot into the glass slipper, and stood up.

Held the foot out to show the messenger.

Who failed to offer her his arm.

Stepped back from her, in fact.

Away. Up. Screams in the hall. The floor rose like a wave. Slammed like a door.

She wept, and the stepsister wiped her poor right foot with water and wrapped it tightly in her own clean petticoat, which she ripped out from under her skirts with no thought for the messenger's presence. In her hand the stepsister held the glass slipper, now smeared with red blood at its heel and black with blood at its toe.

"What have you done, my daughters?" their mother wept.

"The disgrace!" cried the Stepfather.

"Give it to me, girl," the messenger said to the stepsister, but she did not obey. She put her own right foot into the glass slipper, without rising from her place beside Yetiffe on the floor where Yetiffe lay with a cushion under her head, which flamed. The stepsister brought the slipper's mate out from under her apron, and put that one on her left foot.

The messenger knelt before her, as if to a queen.

The stepsister turned to Yetiffe. "I didn't mean . . . ," she said.

"I never thought . . . ," she said to Lysette.

"I'm so sorry," she said, and she was weeping. She knew that they were foolish, and vain, and greedy, and had no kindness for her, but she had always known that, long before she went unbidden to the ball. Her grief when they buried Yetiffe was sharp; her sorrow lasted a long time.

After she had married the Prince, with Lysette as an attendant who, although she could never dance again because of her maimed right foot, could move at a stately pace in the bridal procession, the stepsister invited Lysette to live with her in the palace until such time as she herself should wed, which, in due course, she did, to a privy minister. Lysette had her own salon then, where significant talk—of statecraft and diplomacy, economics and sometimes poetry or painting—was the order of the evenings, to which only a select few were summoned. Never was the name of poor, foolish Yetiffe mentioned, who did not know enough to cauterize a wound. Often, it was not possible to include the dear Prince and the dear Princess in these gatherings. Lysette and her husband were in constant attendance at the palace, however, their presence requested for every occasion, from the birthday parties of the little princes and princesses to the most formal receptions for visiting royalties. No occasion would be the same without her, the young Queen frequently remarked, and Lysette did not disagree.

CORNELIA FUNKE

ROSANNA

Rosanna had an admirer, and he was the strongest boy in her class. Every day after school he would wait exactly where Rosanna took the shortcut through the meadows and he would threaten to hit her if she didn't give him a kiss right away—on the mouth, of course.

Rosanna did not feel like kissing the thug, but she also did not want to give up on her wonderful shortcut.

So she said, "Go away, you meatball, or I will get my big brother. He is much stronger than you. He'll need just one hand to throw you into the stingy nettles."

Sadly, that fattest of all fat lies did not impress the beefcake at all.

"Yeah, right, sugarface," he said with a nasty grin. "You don't even have a big brother."

And Rosanna, her face burning, had no choice but to turn around and walk the long and terribly boring way back home.

For Rosanna did actually have an older brother, but he was completely useless as a defender. His name was Boris and he was exactly one inch shorter than Rosanna. He was also as thin as a straw and more frightened than a rabbit. It really was enough to drive anyone up the wall!

She could do nothing.

Absolutely nothing.

Until one morning, when she saw an advertisement on the back page of the newspaper her father was, as usual, holding up in front of her nose during breakfast: "Professor Ferdinand Flimfaker makes your lies come true," it said clearly in fat print. And beneath, a little smaller, was an address.

So Rosanna stuffed all her savings into her pockets, and after school she set off. Professor Flimfaker lived in a house behind the park, right up on the highest floor. Rosanna counted 123 steps until she finally stood in front of his apartment door. There was no buzzer, just a big iron ring that Rosanna barely managed to reach, even when she stood on her toes. She knocked the iron ring against the door. Dong-dong, it echoed through the stairwell.

The door opened and a tall, thin man looked down at Rosanna with a smile.

"I saw your ad in the newspaper," she said.

"Oh yes?" the professor said. "And what kind of lie did you come to see me about? Emergency lie, bragging lie, school-report lie, consolation lie . . ."

"I'd say a protection lie," Rosanna answered.

"Ah!" said the professor. "Those are the most interesting kind. Please, come in."

He led Rosanna into a room with two green chairs standing

next to a table with a lightbulb in the middle. Underneath the table lay a bright yellow dragon.

"Don't let him disturb you," the professor said. "He's one of my lies, very friendly, and mostly very tired." The dragon opened one eye. Rosanna sat down and told the professor about her problem.

"Goodness me, that really is quite a brazen fellow!" he said. "But you know, the lie about the big brother is used quite often and it only works very rarely. I am guessing you don't have a big brother, do you?"

"I do!" Rosanna said with a sigh. "But he is not strong at all and not a bit violent."

"Hmm, I understand," the professor said. "There is no problem making your lie come true, then, but are you sure you really want such a strong and aggressive brother?"

"Of course!" Rosanna called out.

The professor nodded. "And your brother knows about this, right?" he said.

"O-Of course!" Rosanna lied, and the lightbulb on the table lit up.

Luckily, the professor seemed not to have noticed it. "Fine," he said. "And for how long should your lie become true?"

"Well, forever!" Rosanna answered, surprised.

"In that case I would have to refuse," the professor said. "Shall we say one week to start with? Agreed?"

During dinner Rosanna noticed not one change in her brother. He told his bad jokes and she still had to laugh at them, and later, when they watched television, he covered his eyes during the scary parts.

Rosanna was so angry, she could barely sleep the whole night. The professor had cheated her. He had lied to her, taken her for a fool.

The next morning, Boris was three inches taller than she was. After breakfast already nearly six inches. At least.

"How the boy is growing all of a sudden!" Rosanna's mother said.

And Rosanna was thrilled.

By evening Boris was incredibly big and strong. And aggressive. Instead of telling her jokes, he kicked Rosanna's shin under the table, and he kept calling her "Peewee."

"Can you walk home with me tomorrow after school?" Rosanna asked, rubbing her shin. "I could come and pick you up from your class."

"No way!" Boris muttered. "That would be, like, so embarrassing, to be picked up by such a midget."

Something was going wrong.

"Do your sister a favor, will you?" their mother said, smiling adoringly up at her huge son.

"Fine!" Boris grumbled. "But only this once, okay?"

When the strongest boy in Rosanna's class saw her big brother, his grin just grew even wider.

"Hey, sugarface, you really do have a big brother. Doesn't he have anything better to do than to play bodyguard for little girls?"

"Bodyguard? Me?" Boris growled, and he quickly shoved Rosanna out of his way. "Do I look like I have nothing better to do?"

That was too much. Rosanna stuck her tongue out at the two giants and then she ran away.

"You have to turn him back into a lie!" Rosanna shouted as she sat panting on Professor Flimfaker's green chair. "Please!"

"I feared as much!" the professor answered. "As I said, the big-brother lie rarely works. But there might be another lie . . ."

"Which one?" Rosanna asked.

"I am sorry, but you do have to make up your own lies," the professor answered. "But be warned. Your next lie will stay true all your life!"

Rosanna racked her brain for three days and three nights.

Then, on the fourth day, she again stood in front of Professor Flimfaker's door.

"I got it!" she said—and then she lied until the lightbulb on the professor's table nearly exploded.

"Hey, Rosanna!" the strongest boy in Rosanna's class said the next day. "How about my kiss for today?"

Instead of an answer, Rosanna just gently took him by his collar and lifted him high up into the air. For a few moments she held him above a patch of stingy nettles, and then she placed him neatly on the path behind her.

"Until next time," she said. Whistling, she skipped away from him.

For she was, freshly lied, the strongest girl in the world.

Scorched earth in Darfur, where 3,300 villages were destroyed or damaged.
Photo Credit (both): *UNHCR / K. McKinsey*

NIKKI GIOVANNI

I WISH I COULD LIVE
(IN A BOOK)

I wish I could live
In a book
All wrapped up
In my fairy
God-mother's arms
Or sitting with my Cave
Mother baking dinosaur
Eggs

If I lived
In a book
I could fly
With Ali Baba
And even though it's not right
To steal
The Forty Thieves are
Pretty cool

Maybe there would be
A book about me
One day
Just a little girl being brave
In a world where water
Is in short supply
But everybody
Has a gun

I don't think
That's a good idea
I'd rather be in
A book
Making biscuits
On the frontier
Running with the wind
Following very lightly
On the laughter of the Prairie Dogs

That would be so nice
I think
Living in a book

R. L. STINE

FUNNY THINGS

My friend Brad and I decided to do funny things around the neighborhood because we were bored.

We lived on a block of tiny redbrick houses and square front yards. The houses on the next block were a lot bigger, and the lawns stretched like football fields. Behind our houses—nothing but woods.

I guess you could say we were both poor. But since we were only ten, we didn't think about that stuff too much.

My dad worked at a company that repairs farm machinery. My mom was a secretary in an office downtown.

Brad's parents owned an eyeglass store near the mall. He said they were thinking of closing it down and trying something else.

So guess what? Owen Millard and Brad Lindsay did not hang with the rich kids at school.

When summer came, the other kids all went off to summer

camp or joined a swim club or took off on long vacations with their families.

Brad and I tried to find things to do around the neighborhood. And we tried to keep away from Sid Harcher, our enemy. Sid was a supervillain with amazing powers to make Brad and me mad and frightened.

He could hurt us with his fists of concrete. Or just bump us hard with his stomach of steel, and make us ache for days.

Brad and I aren't giants like Sid. We're probably the shrimpiest guys in fifth grade. We haven't had our growth spurts yet. I think Sid had his growth spurt when he was two or three.

Sid must like us a lot. Why else would he always be teasing us and bumping us and testing out his fists on us?

On a hot August day, the trees shimmered in the yellow sunlight all down our block. Next door, a sprinkler on Mrs. Farraday's front lawn made a *shh shh shh* sound as it sent a spray of water dancing over the grass.

I heard little kids laughing and splashing around in a plastic inflatable pool in Mr. Mellon's backyard. Sadie, the Mellons' big Doberman, sat up and watched Brad and me as we walked past the front yard.

I had my eyes on the dog and walked right into Big Sid. "Oww!" I bounced off as if I'd run into a brick wall.

Sid laughed. His blue eyes flashed. His curly blond hair gleamed in the sunlight. He had a milk mustache, but I wasn't going to be the one to tell him.

Sid is like a different breed. Brad and I are thin and dark-haired and we both wear glasses. He's like a huge, big-pawed golden Lab, and we're miniature dachshunds or maybe Chihuahuas, the hairless, quivering kind.

"Where you two going, Owen?" he asked. "The kiddie swings at the playground?"

That's a typical Sid joke. The best thing to do is to laugh at it, which Brad and I did.

"Just hanging," I said. "You know. Like always."

"Where you going, Sid?" Brad asked.

Sid puffed out his chest. The front of his T-shirt read: MY MOM THINKS I'M GREAT.

Only Sid would be brave enough to wear a T-shirt that lame. But he knew he was safe. He knew no one would make fun of it.

"Got a job. Mowing lawns." He pulled a fly from his curly hair, squeezed it flat, then tossed it to the sidewalk. "You should mow lawns," he said. "Build up your biceps and triceps."

"I get too sweaty," I said. I hate to sweat. I don't understand people who like it.

"Come with me. I'll give you a break," Sid said. "They've got two mowers. I'll share the job. You do the back, and I'll do the front."

"No way," Brad and I said together.

We knew what he wanted. He wanted us to mow both lawns for him. Then he'd grab the money and keep it all.

"We've got to get going," I said.

That's when Sid grabbed our heads and smacked them together like he was trying to crack open coconuts. Pain made my ears ring. I was so dizzy, I couldn't tell the ground from the sky.

"Hey, Sid—why'd you do that?" I cried, rubbing my aching head.

"That's for forgetting my birthday present," Sid replied.

"Wh-when's your birthday?" Brad stammered.

"Tomorrow," Sid said.

"But . . . how do you know we forgot to get you a present?" I asked.

Sid bumped me hard with his chest. "That was *in case* you forget my present. Here's another reminder."

He grabbed for our heads. But Brad and I ducked away from him and took off. We ran full speed around the side of the Mellons' house and headed toward the woods. We didn't even look back to see if Sid was coming after us. He wasn't.

We stopped just inside the trees, breathing hard. We both burst out laughing. I guess because we got away from Sid that time.

Then I saw the big bird's nest on the ground. I almost stepped into it. I stopped myself just in time.

It was an awesome nest. The sticks and twigs and bits of grass were twined together so tightly. It was perfectly round, about the size of a lunch plate. And about three or four inches tall.

I peered inside it. No eggs or little birds or anything. Then I stared up at the tree branches above us. "Must have fallen off that tree," I said, pointing.

That's when I got the idea for the first funny thing.

It just flashed into my mind. A picture of the mailbox at the bottom of Sid's driveway. It was wood and shaped like a bird. I mean, it had a green-and-red parrot's head at the front and blue tail feathers sticking out the back.

I guess Sid's parents like birds, because they have a mailbox that looks like a fat bird. I turned to Brad, who was bent over studying a small hole dug in the grass by a mole or a mouse or something.

"Let's put this nest in Sid's mailbox," I said.

He gazed up at me. "Why?"

"Because it will be funny," I said. "See? A bird mailbox? You open it up and there's a bird's nest inside?"

He snickered. "It's kind of funny."

So we did it. I carefully carried the nest to Sid's driveway. We made sure Sid was off mowing lawns. And we stuffed the nest into the mailbox and shut the door.

We giggled a lot as we hurried away. I told you we were having a boring summer. So playing a prank like this was a big deal.

And it gave us the idea to do more funny things. We didn't cause any damage or give anyone real trouble. We didn't do any harm. We just did some things that made us giggle. You know. Funny things.

We went to Sutter's, the pet shop a few blocks from school. And we bought twelve goldfish. They were only thirty cents each.

We carried them in plastic bags filled with water. The fish gazed out at us with their buggy black eyes.

We waited till the Mellons' two little kids went into their house for lunch. Then we crept across their backyard and dumped the twelve fish into their plastic inflatable pool.

The fish looked like sparkly jewels as they swam in circles in the round pool.

Brad and I hurried away. In my backyard, we collapsed onto the grass and laughed like lunatics. I know. It wasn't *that* funny.

But can you imagine those kids coming out to their pool and finding it filled with fish? Can you imagine how confused their parents will be?

Funny, right?

We were still laughing when Lydia Parks appeared. Lydia lives on the corner. We've known her since first grade. She has cocoa-colored skin, big brown eyes, and ties her black hair into a single braid behind her head.

She was wearing a sleeveless pink shirt over white tennis shorts.

"What's so funny?" she asked. She has a hoarse, froggy-type voice that makes her sound tough, even though she isn't.

"We've been doing some funny things," I said.

She narrowed her eyes at me. "Like what?"

"Can't tell you," I said. "They're secret funny things."

She raised both hands. "Even if I tickle you?" she said.

That made my skin prickle. I'm the most ticklish person on earth. Even *thinking* about tickling makes my skin crawl.

"Owen can't tell you and neither can I," Brad said. "A secret is a secret—right?"

"Wrong," Lydia said. She dove onto me, dug her fingers into my ribs, and started tickling like crazy.

I howled like a wild animal. That's when I decided Brad and I had to do a funny thing to Lydia.

She tickled me until I couldn't breathe. But I didn't tell her our secret. Finally, she gave up and stomped away. "You're both babies," she muttered. She hates it when we don't tell her things.

Brad and I started to think hard. We had to find something funny to do to Lydia.

We walked down the street. It was hard to walk. My ribs ached from all the tickling.

I stopped in front of Mr. Farraday's house. I saw his red wheelbarrow on the driveway. And then I saw a tall ladder leaning against the side of the house.

"Help me," I said to Brad. "I have a funny idea."

We took the ladder and leaned it against the tall tree in the middle of the yard. Then I climbed up and Brad shoved the wheelbarrow up to me.

He pushed and I pulled, and we heaved the wheelbarrow onto a high tree branch. I balanced it carefully to make sure it would stay up there. Then we returned the ladder to the side of the house.

We stopped for a few seconds to catch our breath and to admire our work. I tried to imagine how surprised Mr. Farraday would be when he found his wheelbarrow high in the tree.

Funny. Very funny.

Next we had to find something for Lydia. Brad and I made our way back into the woods. We followed the twisting dirt path deep into the trees. And in a small clearing of tall weeds, we found the perfect thing.

It was tucked in the weeds and high grass, nearly hidden in the long shadow of an old tree. A tiny dollhouse.

Actually, it looked more like a log cabin. It was a wreck. Almost falling apart. Holes in the pointed roof. Green moss growing down one wall.

I bent down, picked it up, and shook it. Empty.

But then I had the strangest feeling. The back of my neck prickled. Was someone watching us?

I jumped to my feet, holding the little cabin in both hands. I gazed all around. "Brad, do you see anyone?"

He shook his head. "Owen, what are you going to do with that little cabin?"

I grinned at him. "You know the big dollhouse Lydia has in her room? The big fancy white dollhouse with all that little furniture inside?"

"Yeah. I've seen it," Brad said. "She loves that dollhouse. She's always saving up money to buy stuff for it."

I nodded. "Well, we're going to switch dollhouses. Put this dirty cabin in her room and take hers away."

Brad frowned. "Think Lydia will think that's funny?"

"I think it's funny," I said. "I'm laughing already. Besides, we'll give her back her real dollhouse tomorrow. After she begs."

So we carried the beat-up little log cabin to Lydia's house. The afternoon sun was sinking. The shadows were getting longer. The air grew cooler.

Brad and I got lucky. We watched from across the street as Lydia and her family piled into their car and drove away. Guess they were going somewhere for dinner.

That made the dollhouse switch very easy. Lydia's parents never lock their back door. We carried the cabin into their kitchen. It smelled of chocolate. I saw a stack of brownies on a plate.

I set the cabin down on the floor next to Lydia's big white dollhouse. Then Brad and I hoisted up the big dollhouse and, carrying it between us, took it to my house.

Easy, right? And funny.

But after that is when the bad stuff started to happen.

Late that night, I was in bed with my eyes wide open. I couldn't get to sleep. I kept thinking about the funny things Brad and I had done all day. And I kept trying to picture Lydia's face when she walked into her room and saw that dirty, crumbling little cabin.

Yawning, I finally started to feel sleepy. I sank my head into the pillow and shut my eyes.

But I opened them when I heard a scraping sound by the window. I squinted into the dim light from the street. The curtains were blowing into the room from a strong breeze.

I started to settle back. But I heard a *thump*. And then rapid thumps. Footsteps? Did something drop in through the window?

I sat up. My heart started to flutter in my chest. Suddenly, I was totally alert.

I felt a tug on my blanket. Another tug. Harder.

"Hey—what's going on?" I said out loud. My voice came out hoarse and weak.

And then something plopped into my bed. Something had climbed my blanket and now it stepped across the bed—*until it was standing on my chest!*

"Ohhh." A frightened moan escaped my throat. I grabbed the blanket with both hands. And stared.

Stared at a little creature. No. A tiny man. No.

He was less than a foot tall. He had a round, bald head no bigger than a tennis ball, and pointy ears. I saw a V-shaped beard under his chin.

His round eyes glowed in the dim light. He wore a diaper-like thing that appeared to be woven out of grass or weeds. His chest was bare and smooth as baby skin.

"Wh-who are you?" I managed to choke out. "What do you w-want?"

His bare feet prickled my chest. He moved up close to my face. His expression turned angry. His eyes glowed coldly.

"Where is my house?" he rasped. Spit formed on the sides of his mouth when he talked.

"Excuse me?" I gasped.

"My house," he rumbled. "I want my house."

I tried to sit up. But he was surprisingly heavy on my chest. "Who are you?" I repeated.

"You might call me an imp," he said. "I believe that's your word for me. My name is Seelum. I am an imp. A very angry imp. I want my house."

I finally realized what he meant. The little cabin. It must be his house.

"I . . . know where it is," I said. "I can get it for you."

He grabbed my hand with both of his. His hands felt hard, strong as metal. He squeezed my skin till it hurt.

"Bring it to me," he rasped. "Return my house to the woods."

"Now?" I cried. "It's late. It's dark. I—I—"

"Now," he said, squeezing my hand again. "Bring my house to the woods, and I'll give you three wishes."

I nearly choked. I couldn't catch my breath. Fear, I guess. Or maybe I was in shock.

"You'll give me three wishes?"

"If you bring my house now," he said.

"Okay," I said. "No problem."

He slid down the bedcovers and scrambled to the open window. I watched him climb up the curtains. His pointed beard gleamed in the moonlight.

He gave me one last glance. Then he dove through the window and disappeared.

I realized I was shivering. My teeth were chattering. I took a deep breath and held it. But I couldn't stop my shakes.

Did I say it would be *no problem* to get the little guy's house back?

I leaped out of bed, crossed the room to my closet, and pulled on clothes I'd left in a heap on the floor. I glanced at my bed table clock—nearly one in the morning.

My first problem was sneaking out of the house without my parents catching me. The stairs creaked and groaned if you put one foot on them. But I had no choice. I couldn't leap out the window like that imp.

I lifted myself onto the banister, leaned forward—and slid downstairs. Much quieter—except for the *thud* I made when I hit the floor.

Holding my breath, I tiptoed to the front door. It made a soft click as I pulled it open. I slid outside and closed it silently behind me.

Okay. Step one. I made it out of the house. So far, so good. If only I could stop the shakes.

It was a hot, steamy night. The wind had died. The tall trees stood perfectly still. Nothing moved. The little houses on my block were all dark.

The front lawn sparkled from a heavy dew. A rabbit standing on the grass saw me and froze. It was all so still. Not even cricket sounds. It felt like I was in a dream.

But I knew it was real. I had to sneak into Lydia's house. Creep into her room. Grab the little cabin and run.

I've never sneaked into anyone's house before, day or night. What if her parents heard me moving around in the dark and thought I was a burglar? What would they do?

I didn't want to think about it. I didn't want to think about anything. I felt like that rabbit on my lawn, frozen in terror.

I thought of calling Brad. But he had to be sound asleep. And he couldn't really help me. I had to do this on my own.

Somehow I walked to Lydia's house. I tried to keep in the deep shadows of the overhanging trees. My heart was beating hard as I crept up her driveway.

Whoa. Hold on. I glanced at the empty drive. No car.

I let out a long whoosh of air. Her family wasn't home. Sometimes they drove to Lydia's aunt's house and stayed overnight.

Maybe I caught a break. I tried the back door. Still unlocked.

I stepped into the kitchen. No sign that anyone had been there. The plate of brownies hadn't been touched.

I wanted to jump up and down and cheer. No one home! That made my job a lot easier. I hurried up to Lydia's room. I didn't even bother to be quiet.

It was hard to see. The curtains were drawn. It was nearly pitch black. But I knew where I'd left the little wood cabin.

A few seconds later, I had it in my hands. A few seconds after that, I was running down Lydia's driveway, carrying it in front of me.

My sneakers slapped the pavement. Then I turned and ran along the side of a house toward the woods. "Whoooa!" I slipped on the dewy grass and almost fell face forward onto the cabin.

Luckily, I caught my balance and kept moving. The crickets started up as I reached the edge of the woods. The shrill sound rang in my ears.

I stopped and glanced around. The trees were like a dark wall, high above my head. I'd never been in the woods in the middle of the night. What kind of creatures came out at night? How would I ever find the imp?

I took a few steps on the path. Narrow beams of yellow moonlight lit my way. I took a few more steps, the crickets rasping in my ears.

I gasped as the imp stepped out from behind a fallen tree. The moon gleamed off his bald head. His bare shoulders and chest were yellow in the moonlight.

"I . . . I brought your house," I said breathlessly.

He gazed up at me, hands on the waist of his diaper. "Where? Where is it?"

"Here." I shoved the cabin at him.

To my surprise, he shook his head and spit on the ground. Then he gazed up at me, his face twisted in anger. "Idiot!" he cried. "That's not my house!"

"N-not your house?" I stammered. The cabin fell from my hands. It hit the ground and broke into a hundred pieces.

"Fool! That doesn't even *look* like my house!" the imp screamed. He kicked my ankle with his bare foot.

I jumped back. His foot was too tiny to hurt me.

He kicked me again. "My house! My house! Where is my house?" He was screaming at the top of his lungs.

"Okay," I said. "You need a time-out. Just take a deep breath. I think I know where your house is."

"Bring it to me! *Now!*" He tried to kick my ankle. Slipped in the dirt. And landed on his back.

I didn't wait for him to get up. I ran through the trees and out of the woods. I was pretty sure I knew what his house was. I ran without stopping all the way to the mailbox where Brad and I had stashed the nest.

Was it still inside? I pulled down the lid. Yes!

Carefully, I eased the nest out of the mailbox. The twigs and weeds scratched my hands. I held it tightly. I knew it was delicate. I had to get it back to that angry imp in one piece.

My shoes slipped on the wet grass again. I half walked, half ran back to the woods. My heart was racing. This *had* to be his house. It *had* to.

He was waiting for me on the path, hands on his waist, tapping one bare foot on the dirt.

"Is this . . . is this your house?" I stammered.

"Of course it is," he snapped. "Put it down on the ground and scram out of here."

I set the nest down. He climbed into it and marched back and forth. Testing it, I guess.

"Beat it, kid," he growled. He made a nasty face. Then he spit over the side of the nest.

I leaned over him. "You're forgetting something," I said. "Remember? You promised me three wishes?"

He spit again. He just missed my shoe. "Take a walk, kid. And don't steal anyone's house on your way home."

"But—what about my three wishes?" I asked in a shaky voice.

He shook his bald head. "I'm an imp. I don't grant wishes. I don't know how."

I blinked. "You mean you lied?"

He nodded. "Yeah. Imps lie a lot. What grade did *you* get in imp history?"

"I didn't take imp history," I said. "I can't believe you lied to me."

He shrugged his slender shoulders. "That's the breaks, I guess. I don't have any wish powers, kid. My only power is to change humans into imps."

I leaned closer. "Really? You can do that?"

A thin-lipped grin spread over his face. "Yeah. It's easy. Like *that*." He snapped his tiny fingers. "Shut your eyes, kid. I'll turn you into an imp. But you'll have to build your own house. I don't share."

"Uh . . . no! No, thanks!" I screamed. "But I have an idea."

I reached down, wrapped my fingers around his waist, and picked him up.

"Put me down!" he screamed. "Put me down—*now*! I'll turn you into an imp. I swear!"

"Just be patient," I told him. "I have a very funny idea."

• • •

The next afternoon, Brad and I walked up to Big Sid Harcher's house and rang the doorbell. I could hear music inside and kids talking and laughing.

After a few seconds, Sid opened the door and poked his big blond head out. "What do you two geeks want?" he snarled. "Don't try to crash my birthday party. You're definitely not invited."

"We know," I said. "But we didn't forget your present."

I shoved the brightly gift-wrapped box toward Sid's hands. I could feel the imp bouncing around inside.

Sid squeezed the box in both hands and shook it. "This better be good," he said. He slammed the door shut before Brad or I could say happy birthday.

We laughed all the way to my house.

Maybe the angry imp would change Big Sid into an imp. Or maybe he wouldn't.

But either way, it was a funny thing.

MARILYN NELSON

CAUTIOUS WISHING

Say you've trapped an elf or caught a magic fish:
Beware of greed, ambition, and desire.
When it offers you anything your heart can wish,
just free it. Because wishes can backfire.

If you wish every meal will be a sumptuous feast,
you could wind up having to diet to lose weight.
If you wish unwisely, in anger, or in haste,
you just might destroy every good thing you create.

We're all living with side effects unforeseen
by the science that wished us forward toward new frontiers.
The thirteen-year-olds who wished they were nineteen
are too soon fifty, lamenting the passing years.

And the girl who wished her golden retriever could talk
has to listen to his detailed monologue
about pees and poops he encounters on every walk.
Because a talking dog is still a dog.

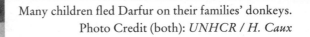

Many children fled Darfur on their families' donkeys.
Photo Credit (both): *UNHCR / H. Caux*

FRANCISCO X. STORK

THE RULES FOR WISHING

I

Dear Pablito:

Happy Birthday. I can't believe you're fifteen now.
I know your birthday is not for another month, but I
don't know how long it takes for a letter to get to you.
Sometimes the letters sit up there in the warden's office
for weeks while they get read and inspected. I'm sending
you fifty dollars for your birthday. It's most all I earned
except for what I kept for cigarettes. I've been trying
to quit but it's very hard on account of the boredom. I
know I say this in every letter, but I wish you'd write to
me. Even just a note to let me know the money got to
you safely. I'm afraid the guards in the warden's office
may stash the bills in their pockets. I have no way of
knowing. Just let me know you got the money. That
would mean a lot to me. Remember if you can that your

mama needs you. I'm just asking for some little sign that you know I'm alive. As for me, I'm doing okay. I'm doing a good job working at the printing shop. The head trustee told me if I keep up the good work, pretty soon I'll be getting a raise to three dollars a day. I'll be able to send you a little more. I got a letter from Sherry B. She tells me you don't talk much and that you spend all your time alone. That worries me a lot. You don't know how bad I feel I can't be with you.

I need to go now. I hope you write me just a tiny note.

Love you.

Mama

II

Pablo manages to hide the letter under the sheets just as the door opens. Mrs. W peeps in and smiles. It is hard to interpret that smile. It could be that she likes waking kids up at 5:30 A.M. or it could be that she's happy. She's the kind of person that wakes up happy. Pablo can tell by the sunken space on her upper lip that she has forgotten her front teeth. According to Breaker-Breaker, Mrs. W lost her teeth when Dennis, a kid that lived at the farm a couple of years ago, punched her in the mouth. Sherry B denies this story. She says that Mrs. W's teeth fell out of their own accord, probably from eating the wretched taffy she loves so much.

Mrs. W soaks her dentures in a cream-colored tub that used to hold margarine. She keeps the tub with the teeth in her own private bathroom that no one is supposed to enter, except that

everyone sneaks up there when Mrs. W is not looking. Pablo
goes in there to steal aspirin or to take swigs of Pepto-Bismol.
There's a closet in that bathroom that holds all the emergency
supplies: a red hot-water bottle, Band-Aids of different shapes,
a bottle of alcohol that is now empty because Breaker-Breaker
drank the original contents, glycerine suppositories, a box of
sanitary napkins that get dispensed to Sherry B once a month.

"Oh good, ure up." It is difficult for Mrs. W to enunciate
without her teeth. "Is ure durn doo meek de cows." It is Pablo's
turn to milk the cows. As if he didn't know. He nods. She is still
at the door, perhaps expecting to catch a glimpse of him in his
underwear. Breaker-Breaker swears from "personal experience"
that Mrs. W likes young blood. But who can believe what
Breaker-Breaker says?

She finally turns around slowly and leaves. She's headed back
in the direction of her bathroom, hopefully to glue her teeth
back in. He swings his legs over the side of the bed. The first
thing he does is put the folded letter inside his *Count of Monte
Cristo* book. The book is lying on the floor next to the bed
where he dropped it just before he fell asleep. He places the
book in the top drawer of the dresser. Then he takes off his
T-shirt, folds it, and places it under the pillow. He only wears
the orange University of Texas T-shirt at night. It's true that it
hasn't been washed in months, but how dirty can a T-shirt get
if all you do is sleep in it? He remembers suddenly last night's
dream and how his body burned with sweat. He quickly shakes
this memory away. It's good that he can do that, shake memo-
ries away. Sometimes they get stuck and do their dirty grind
until they have their fill.

He puts on the blue jeans and the gray T-shirt that he always wears. Mrs. W makes him wash these once a week whether they are dirty or not. While he's tying on his red sneakers, he thinks of the letter he just folded. Why did Sherry B say that he wasn't talking much? He talks enough. As needed. What more is there to say? Forget that. Why did Sherry B write his mother? He hasn't felt anger in a long time, but he feels it now.

He walks down the stairs and goes out the front door quickly. He wants to be out there before the other three are up. The other three are Breaker-Breaker, Rolando and Sherry B. Breaker-Breaker and Rolando share a room. Sherry B has her own room. Sherry B's room has an empty bed and Mrs. W told them that another girl is coming in a few days. Sherry B is not happy about that. She likes being the only female in the house. Mrs. W doesn't count. Breaker-Breaker says Mrs. W has been neutered. The whole group semi-agrees with Sherry B, about the new girl, that is. They are all fearful of someone new coming. The wrong person can stink up the whole place. "Even if she's hotter than hot, if she's got the wrong attitude, it's bad news." That's what Breaker-Breaker says.

The truth is that the present group is not all perfect. Breaker-Breaker especially with his ongoing addiction to alcohol is problematic. Heck, everyone has problems. But all things considered, the farm is not a bad place and everyone knows that. You milk cows, shovel manure and other kinds of animal poop, feed chickens and turkeys and sheep and hogs, and hoe and plant and water and weed, and it's still not a bad place. For Pablo, the farm is good because he's left alone. More or less. And he has his own room.

It's a small room, really. It fits a bed, a dresser, a desk, a chair, and a bedside table. The room has one small window that looks out into the barn. The room is so small that it must have been a storage closet at some point. It's perfect as far as Pablo is concerned. Its tightness is comforting. Its very smallness serves as protection against the recurring dream.

The farm has two cows—Josephine and Magda. For some reason no one calls them Josie and Maggie. This could have something to do with their disposition, which is grumpy. They like to whack whoever is milking them with their tail under the pretense that they are swatting flies. Josephine is Magda's mother, but you'd never know it. Whenever possible, Josephine bites Magda in the rump.

It took a while for Pablo to learn how to handle the cow's teats. At the beginning he'd squeeze and pull but could never get a consistent flow going. It was Sherry B who finally showed him how to master the technique. The movement of the thumb, index finger, and hand required a combination of tenderness and strength. The milk is like a child too shy to come out and play. You have to coax it out tenderly, firmly. Except for Sherry B, Pablo is the best milker in the farm. Not that Josephine and Magda ever appreciate him.

He gets a half a pail from Josephine and is moving on to Magda in the next stall when he hears someone behind him. It is Sherry B.

"You were talking to yourself again last night," she says to him. Sherry B's room is next to his and noises can be heard through the wall. Pablo himself has heard the smooth rustle of Sherry B taking off her blue jeans. Sherry B is almost sixteen, taller than everyone in the farm except Pablo. She has short brown hair that she insists on cutting herself and so her head looks like a badly mowed lawn. She has eyes that change tint from light brown to dark green depending on the time of day and bushy eyebrows that give her an intense, concentrated look. She is beautiful but rough. Someone you would like to pet but don't.

"I wasn't talking," Pablo says. He places the pail on the cement ledge that separates the stalls and covers it with a piece of white cloth to keep the flies away.

Sherry B removes the cloth, dips a finger in the milk, and licks it. "Don't worry, I washed my hands."

"I wasn't worried." Pablo never drinks the milk. It makes his chronic upset stomach worse.

"Want to know what you were saying?"

"Don't you got to feed the chickens or something?" Pablo is now in Magda's stall. He'd rather not talk to Sherry B. He yanks Magda's tail to let her know that he does not want to get whacked while he is milking. He sits on the three-legged wooden stool and begins to squirt milk into the tin pail. Vapor rises from the warm milk.

Sherry B leans back against the ledge. "You know what's so strange about you?"

Pablo shakes his head. He doesn't want to know. To get a good milking rhythm going requires focus. He doesn't think he can listen to Sherry B and milk at the same time. Sherry B likes to psychoanalyze people. She is forever offering up her theories as to why people behave this way or that.

Sherry B goes on. "You give this appearance of being in another world and yet you're aware of all these details. Like right then, you remembered this was my week to feed the chickens."

"Shhh. I'm trying to milk."

"You're pulling too hard. You're hurting her. Breasts are very sensitive, even in cows."

Pablo instinctively turns his head and looks first at Sherry B's face and then at her small breasts. He didn't mean to be so forward. Sherry B crosses her arms. He remembers at that moment what Breaker-Breaker said about Sherry B one time when they were out in the field cutting alfalfa: "She's been around the block, that's for damn sure." That's what Breaker-Breaker said.

"What? Why are you looking at me like that?" Sherry B almost shouts.

"Nothing." Pablo goes back to the milking and tries to recover the rhythm he's lost.

"Who's Lupy?" she says to him after a while.

He stops and looks at her, a stunned look on his face.

"That's what you were talking about last night. Or maybe it was early this morning because you woke me up. You were carrying on this big conversation. I couldn't make out most of it, but I did hear something about a Lupy."

"I was just talking in my sleep. It's nonsense." But he is suddenly scared. He thought that the conversation happened silently in the dream and now it turns out the conversation was out loud.

"You kept talking to this Lupy and then you were calling her, 'Lupy! Lupy!' It was sad, like this Lupy was dying or something. Sounded awful. Who's Lupy?"

"No one. It was just a dream," he says, irritated.

"Okay, don't have a cow." She starts to laugh. "What you were saying didn't sound like a regular dream, though. It sounded so real. And anyways, dreams *are* real. They can help us find out what we really want. I mean, it's rare that we should take dreams literally. Lupy could stand for something you wish for deep inside. Do you know anyone named Lupy?"

"I gotta finish milking this cow. She's getting aggravated."

"Here, let me do it. I can talk and milk at the same time. Women are better at multitasking." She stands next to him, bumps him with her thigh.

He tries a few more times to get a flow going, but nothing comes out. He's lost the mental tranquility required for the job. He stands up and lets her have the stool. Quickly, streams of milk start filling the pail. He walks away.

"Don't go," she says. "The least you can do is keep me company while I do your job."

He stops and takes a step toward the ledge that separates the stalls. He leans against it, just like she did. "I don't feel like talking about dreams," he tells her.

"You never feel like talking about anything. Do you, *Pablito*?"

"Don't call me that." He hates it when people call him Pablito. His mother calls him that.

She places her head against Magda's big beige belly. The milk flows effortlessly into the pail. "Gosh, you're so ornery. Did it ever occur to you that people may want to help you? I mean, I know lots about dreams and not only because I did a six-month stint in a mental hospital. Not that it did me any good." She pauses and looks at him, hoping for a smile, but there's no smile on his face. "Anyway, my experience with dreams is that there're two kinds. You got what I call your basic maintenance dreams that happen every night and no one ever remembers. These dreams are just the mind cleaning itself up. Maintenance. Then you got your fix-it dreams. These are the ones you remember because they're trying to tell you something. They're trying to fix something in you that needs fixing. Whatever you had going this morning was a fix-it dream." She stops milking and looks up at him. "Pablo, it wasn't the first time you were talking about Lupy."

Regis, the barn's resident cat, peers in the stall. He comes up to Pablo and rubs his side against his leg. Pablo reaches down and picks him up, strokes him. "So?"

"I guess what I want to tell you is that you shouldn't ignore this . . . dream."

Regis squirms out of his arms and jumps down. He goes to the pail under Magda, meows, and looks up at Sherry B. "He wants some milk," Pablo says. Sherry B absentmindedly dips her finger in the pail and lets Regis lick it.

"It's the same dream you keep having, isn't it?"

He looks away.

She starts milking again and then stops. The pail is almost full. She stands up and looks straight at him. "Pablo, you need to talk to someone about it."

"About what?" He edges away from her.

"About the dream. It's not normal to keep having the same scary dream."

"You're not an expert on normal."

"That's for sure. But I know something about mental states.

I've had a few myself. The mental hospital I was in . . . there were kids there who . . . kids who were afraid to go to sleep at night because of what waited for them there."

"Are you saying I'm crazy?" Anger rises in his voice.

"Crazy? I'd never use that word. That's a word people use to scare other people into being the same. I just think that the brain is like this delicate egg that can crack. Things can happen to a person. A person can see things and feel things that are too strong that crack the egg."

He is silent. An image that he doesn't want to see begins to form inside of him. He shakes his head to brush the image away. He closes his eyes and when he opens them, he feels her hand on his shoulder. "Leave me alone." He doesn't say this with force. He says it as if he were saying the exact opposite.

"Okay."

"And who told you to write my mother?"

"I didn't . . ."

"Yes you did."

"I mean I didn't write to her first. She wrote to me asking about you. 'Cause you never write to her."

She looks at him briefly, brushes Magda's back with her hand. Blood rushes to his face and then drains slowly. He stammers, "She doesn't know you. How does she know you?"

"It could be Mrs. Garret told her, I don't know. I got a letter from your mom, that's all."

Mrs. Garret, otherwise known as the State Lady, comes to the farm every month. She also visits his mother now and then. He stares at Sherry B. Bites his lip. "You shoulda told me!"

She ignores his outburst. "She says she's never once gotten a single letter from you."

"It's none of your business!" he shouts. He sees her eyes redden. He's hurt her. Good. Maybe she'll stay out of his life. He expects her to turn around and leave, but she stays right where she stands.

"Why is your mom in prison?"

"Don't go there," he warns.

"Okay." She backs off. "Can I say just one thing?"

"No."

"Whatever she did, she deserves to be forgiven."

He clenches his jaw, stares at her.

"You should talk about it," she adds.

"No I shouldn't."

"Pablo, here's the thing. You're gonna fall apart. I've seen it all before. I've been there."

She's been around the block. He remembers Breaker-Breaker's words. "Are you finished milking?"

"That's all she gave." Regis is sticking his head in the pail, trying to get at the milk. Sherry B picks up the pail and puts it on the ledge. Regis meows, disappointed. She lowers her head briefly and then speaks. "Okay, I'll let it be. But let me just say this. Everything that happens to us is connected. You not writing to your mom for whatever reason, those terrible nightmares you're having, it's all connected. If you run away from something over here, it will come up someplace else and usually in a worse way."

Pablo can't help grinning. Sometimes Sherry B sounds older than Mrs. W.

"What?" Sherry B asks.

"You learn all this stuff at that mental hospital you were in?"

"Some."

"I better take the milk in and boil it." He goes to grab the pail and she moves out of his way. He's almost out of the barn, the pail dangling in his arm, when she asks again.

"Who's Lupy?"

He hesitates for a second, then keeps on walking. She follows behind him. His first impulse is to ignore her, but then he feels this strange need to speak. The words come out of his mouth almost involuntarily. "Her name is María Guadalupe."

"María Guadalupe," Sherry B repeats.

"Yeah." For someone who doesn't talk much, he has these sudden rushes of verbalization, almost like words have been impatiently waiting years for a chance to come out.

"Who is she?"

He feels suddenly embarrassed and afraid. He has told her way too much. The look of worry on her face tells him this is the case. He hurries away from her and the milk sloshes to the ground.

"Wait, Pablo, wait." She runs up to him and taps his shoulder. He stops. They're halfway between the barn and the house. He feels as if the whole world can see him. She moves in front of him. She's breathing fast. Why is she so interested in him? It's not that she's nosy. It's something else. There's tenderness in her eyes that he has seen before but never imagined it could be for him. Now that tenderness is enveloping him, pulling him in. It's like she wants to feel what he's feeling, even if it's not all that good.

"Here," he says, giving her the pail. "I'll do the chickens if you take this in." He turns around and heads toward the chicken coop before she can say anything.

He opens the door to the shed that serves as a chicken coop and the chickens spill into the yard, cackling. He takes a few handfuls of feed from a container that was once a garbage can and throws them at the chickens. Then he goes inside to collect the eggs.

He's digging under the third roost when she comes in and stands at the entrance, the morning light shining behind her. "So who's Lupy," she asks.

He shakes his head incredulously. "You don't give up, do you?"

"No." She steps into the darkness of the chicken coop.

"Why?"

"Why what?" She picks up a brown egg and places it in the wicker basket hanging on his arm.

"Why are you so interested?"

She looks at him as if that was one of the stupidest questions she's ever been asked. She's obviously not going to answer it, but he waits anyway. "Duh," she finally says. Even in the darkness he can see her face turn red. He turns around, picks up another egg. "Has it ever occurred to you," he hears her say behind him, "that people may care about you? That they may be concerned about you? Did you ever consider that even people like Rolando or Breaker-Breaker, when he's sober enough to notice, may be worried about you? Don't you think most of us have been broken at some point or another or seen kids fall apart and know the signs? This is your first time in a place like this. We've all been in a place like this for the first time. It's not easy. But I'll tell you this. Nobody ever makes it alone." She stops as if she suddenly forgot how to speak, as if she used up all the words she had.

The chicken coop is totally silent. He breathes the ammonia-like smell and for a second he is filled with fear, a strange fear that she will walk out on him and never talk to him again. He turns quickly. She's still there.

"Lupy is my sister," he says. "María Guadalupe. I called her Lupy."

III

It's not really a nightmare because there are no monsters or killings and nobody gets hurt. I've had nightmares before, plenty of them. Once I dreamt that I was standing in a long line of people of all ages and this lady who was dressed in white and whose face was covered with a veil was walking by the people in the line. Every once in a while the lady would stop and smile at someone and it was clear that the lady was death herself and whoever she smiled at was a goner. That was a nightmare. Feeling her walk slowly up the line to where I'm standing, seeing her weird smile through that thick white veil. It was a horrible smile. Not really a smile but not a grin or a smirk either. And I don't know how I could see it, the veil was so thick. I always woke up before she got to me.

The dream with Lupy isn't like that. It's an ordinary dream. Not even a dream, more like a memory. A memory that comes when I'm asleep.

She was a beautiful light-skinned baby. I don't think I've ever seen Mama and Papa so happy as when she was born. Papa even stopped traveling and got a job in construction, right there in Brownsville. He didn't go out at night either like he usually did. He still drank, but at least he did it at home.

I was twelve. Old enough to take care of her and so I did. A couple of months after she was born, Mama put her crib in my room. She said it was because their bedroom didn't get as much ventilation as mine, but I knew that wasn't the reason. The real reason is that Papa got angry when Lupy cried at night. Lupy was colicky. The first nights Mama came over and picked her up when she cried, but I could hear Papa yell when she went back to their room. Papa believed that you spoiled kids if you picked them up when they cried at night.

I think that Lupy and I became so close that year because I went to her and rocked her at the first sound she made, before she started to cry. It was a way to keep the peace in the house, but I didn't mind. I gave her the bottle Mama prepared for her and we'd fall asleep together in the rocking chair.

Then one day, just before her first birthday, I was changing her shirt and I saw the bruises on her arms. They were purple, the size of a man's thumbs. Someone had squeezed her arms as if to shake her. I went to Mama. Papa wasn't there. He had left the day before on one of his trips. He had started traveling again. I found her crying in her bedroom.

"He hurt Lupy, didn't he?" I said to her.

"He didn't do it on purpose," she said. "You know how he gets sometimes."

Yeah, I knew how he got sometimes.

That's about it, really, as far as the dream goes. There's one more scene that happens a couple of months later. I come home from school and look for Lupy but I can't find her. I go to my room and she's not in her bed. We had taken out the crib and put a little bed in there. I go back to the kitchen where Mama's cooking dinner.

"Where's Lupy?" I ask. That's when I see the bottle of tequila next to the refrigerator. Mama didn't even bother to hide it. "Where's Lupy?" I shout at her. Now I know something is wrong.

Mama turns around slowly. Her eyes are steady on me and I know she's been drinking but she's not drunk. She pulls out a kitchen chair and sits down. "I did what was best for her," she says.

In the dream, I keep hearing my mother's words. They come to me garbled like a bad telephone connection: "A nice Anglo couple. She won't lack for anything. You have to understand. Not a good place for her."

That's all. It's not really a nightmare. More like a memory that comes to me when I sleep.

IV

Mrs. W lent us the truck, and we're taking Pablo to the Whataburger in San Benito for his birthday. I'm going to drive because Mrs. W doesn't trust Breaker-Breaker with the truck. She's onto him about the drinking and even though he's been sober for a week, it was still a no go. Breaker-Breaker is eighteen and I have a driver's permit that lets me drive in the company of an adult, so we'll be okay. Assuming no one looks into the question of Breaker-Breaker's supposed adulthood too deeply.

It's going to be just the three of us. Rolando got into a fight after last Friday's football game and is doing time in juvie jail. He was on probation, so there was no question of where he was going if he got into trouble again. The sad part is that, according to Breaker-Breaker, it wasn't his fault. Or at least he didn't start it this time. Breaker-Breaker says he was protecting the cheerleaders.

The amazing thing, the small miracle, is that Pablo has agreed to go. It took a lot of persuading but he finally said okay, probably just to keep me quiet. I knew it was his birthday today because his mother told me in a letter. I started working on him this morning. I followed him out to the barn and as usual waited for him to start milking Josephine.

"Not you again," he says as soon as he sees me.

"Yes, me again," I tell him.

"What now?" He's pretending like he's in a bad mood, but by now I can tell that he isn't. He stops milking. It's a fact. Pablo cannot milk and talk at the same time.

"Guess what day it is today?" I ask him.

"It's just another day," he says, like he doesn't know. Thing is, knowing Pablo, he probably doesn't know.

"It's your birthday!" I say.

"Let me guess. You got another letter from my mother."

"*Correcto mundo,* Pablo." I almost call him Pablito, but I stop myself just in the nick of time.

"What does she say now?" He's just sitting there, holding on to the cow, not even looking at me.

"You ever going to write to her?"

"You ever going to mind your own beeswax?"

I think about it. "No. Not likely. Why is it that you can't talk and milk at the same time? It's not that hard. I'm not exactly taxing your brain with the topic of my conversation."

He looks at me with this stern look on his face. "You wanna milk this cow?"

"Nope. But things would go easier if you could learn to move your lips and your hands at the same time. Think all the talking we could get done while you do your chores."

He shakes his head and tries again. He stops. "It isn't the talking and milking I can't do. It's the *thinking* and milking."

"What's there to think about?"

He's still not looking at me. After a while he says, "For one thing, I'm thinking about what you tell my mother."

"I didn't tell her about your dream, if that's what you're wondering."

I hear him sigh. He gets a couple of puny squirts out of one teat. "Hey," I say. "I'll leave you alone and promise I won't bother you while you're milking if you come to Whataburger with us."

"Us?"

"Yeah, Breaker-Breaker and me want to take you out for your birthday."

"You told Breaker-Breaker that it's my birthday?"

"Yup. And Mrs. W too. The whole world knows. I might put in a call to Rolando this afternoon too. Maybe they'll let me talk to him."

I see the very beginning of a smile.

"Okay, it's set. We leave at five. Mrs. W has okayed the use of the truck."

I'm about to leave when I hear him say, "Wait."

"Yes?"

"How long will you not bother me if I go?"

"What?"

"You promised not to bother me while I was milking if I went. For how long will you not bother me?"

"A week?"

"No."

"No?"

"Forever."

"Forever?" I gulp. "That's a long time."

He shrugs. It's a "take it or leave it" kind of shrug.

"All right," I say. "I won't talk to you while you're milking . . . ever. But that only applies to while you're milking. And that's only because you can't milk and talk at the same time. You're fair game any other time."

He shrugs again. But this time the shrug is accompanied by a full smile.

When we get back from Whataburger, we find Mrs. W putting the finishing touches on a chocolate cake. I'm practically floored because I've never seen Mrs. W bake.

"It's from a box," she says by way of explanation. "And the frosting I got right out of a can. They make it real easy for you these days."

"Mrs. W, is that for *moi*? I didn't even know you cared," Breaker-Breaker says.

"It's for Pablo," Mrs. W says, looking at Pablo. Pablo is

standing in the middle of the kitchen, not knowing where to put his hands. He finally sticks them in his pockets. "Y'all get yourselves some milk and let's have us some cake."

"Now you're talking my language." Breaker-Breaker is already opening the refrigerator, getting out the plastic pitcher of milk. "Wish we had something a little more joyful than milk."

"Don't you start now." Mrs. W glares at Breaker-Breaker.

"Just kidding," he says.

I get four glasses from the cupboard. Pablo looks embarrassed. He was that way at the Whataburger, like it's painful for him to be the center of attention. "Sit," I tell him. He pulls out a kitchen chair and sits on the edge.

Mrs. W is rummaging through a kitchen drawer. "I put them in here someplace."

"What?" I ask.

"Them birthday candles," she says, exasperated.

"I never got no cake or birthday candles," Breaker-Breaker says, pretending he's offended.

"Oh, shush!" Mrs. W says. "If you did your chores the way Pablo does, you mighta gotten one too. Where did I put those candles?"

"We don't need candles," Pablo says. He speaks so softly, Mrs. W doesn't hear him.

"Of course we do," I say to him.

"Where could they be?" Mrs. W asks, bewildered.

"I got some matches in my room. We can use those."

"Why do you have matches in your room?" I ask, as if I didn't know. Alcohol is not the only self-medication that Breaker-Breaker administers to himself.

"I'll go get the matches." Breaker-Breaker shoots out of the kitchen and is leaping up the stairs to his room.

"Where's he going?" Mrs. W asks no one in particular.

"To get matches."

"I have matches. What I need is them candles."

"Let's just have the cake," Pablo says.

"You be quiet. You don't have a say in this," I tell him. I'm already aggravated by the fact that he had to pay for all of us at the Whataburger. Breaker-Breaker, who had promised to pay, conveniently forgot his wallet. Then Breaker-Breaker proceeds to tell us that it's an old Mexican custom for the person having the birthday to treat family and friends to a banquet. As if he would know about Mexican customs. He's whiter than I am.

Breaker-Breaker sticks fifteen wooden matches in the chocolate cake. Mrs. W is still searching in her mind for the candles. "I'm sure I bought some. Didn't I?"

"Forget about the candles, Mrs. W. These will work." I take her by the shoulders and sit her down. Breaker-Breaker is about to light the matches when I stop him. "Wait. Before you light them, Pablo has to think of a wish."

"A wish?" Pablo has no idea what I'm talking about.

"You didn't know that?"

"No," Pablo says.

"Let's go. Let's go." Breaker-Breaker lights a match. I reach out, grab his hand, and blow it out.

"Hold your horses," I tell him. "We gotta get this right. Pablo only gets one wish. He has to make it count." I look into Pablo's eyes and it hits me that he knows nothing about birthday candles and wishes. This could very well be the first time anyone has celebrated his birthday, but I don't want to ask for fear of embarrassing him. "Okay," I say, "here are the rules for making wishes on your birthday. He's going to light the matches. Now, those matches are going to burn down real quick, so it'd be good for you to have your wish ready beforehand. Then, when the candles or matches are lit, you make the wish, close your eyes, and blow all the matches out with one breath. If all the matches go out, your wish is granted. Got that?"

Pablo nods. But he still looks like he has questions.

"What? Tell me." He shakes his head. "All right, close your eyes and make a wish." Pablo shuts his eyes tight. "Light them up," I tell Breaker-Breaker.

When all the matches are lit, Pablo finally opens his eyes and takes a deep breath. I see his lips move for a few seconds, and then in one breath he blows out the matches.

"Yay!" we all yell. All of us except Pablo. I can't tell whether the look on his face is sad or just serious.

After we finish eating cake, Breaker-Breaker and Mrs. W go to the living room to watch *True Crime*, their favorite reality show. I'm washing the dishes we used and Pablo is drying.

"What if you wish for something that's impossible?" he asks out of the blue.

I finish rinsing the dish and then put it in the rack before I answer. "When it comes to wishes, there's no such thing as impossible." I try to sound convincing.

"Do you wanna know what I wished for?" he says after a while.

I think about it. This is a hard question. Pablo never talks about himself and I'm afraid if I say no, I will miss a once-in-a-lifetime opportunity. Still, rules are rules. "I'd like to," I say softly, "but if you tell me, then your wish may not come true. That's one of the rules."

"Oh," he says.

And then it happens. I don't know how it happens but it does. I suddenly know what he wished for. I hear his voice inside of me, the way he called out to her in his dream.

We finish the dishes in silence. All during this time I'm wondering whether it's against the wishing rules if I tell Pablo that I know. Technically, he wouldn't have told me. I decide to take a little chance. Bend the rules a bit.

"Want to go outside?" I ask.

"I gotta go check on the cows anyway," he says.

Outside, the sky is brilliant with stars. That's one of the things about the farm that I like the most. At night you see more stars than you ever knew existed. We walk slowly and quietly toward the barn. His hand touches mine for a brief moment and I lose my breath thinking that he is going to hold it, but it was just an accident.

"That thing you wished for. Maybe it's not as impossible as you think."

He doesn't act surprised at what I say. He stops and looks at me. "You know then?"

"Yes," I tell him. "I know."

"Is it against the rules for you to know?" he asks, smiling.

"I don't think so, as long as we don't say the wish out loud."

He nods. There's an old wooden bench outside the barn. We sit there.

"I miss her," he says.

We are quiet for a long time.

I see a shooting star and make the same wish.

NATE POWELL

CONJURERS

Sixteen-year-old refugee Farihalh wants to become "Minister of Darfur."
Photo Credit: *UNHCR / H. Caux*

Endings are a time for reflection. This collection closes with a story to make you think, not only about its own meaning, but also about how the theme of wishes expressed in each story and poem relates to the refugees this book will help. Even though this story was not written with refugees in mind, it explores things that all of us, even the most vulnerable, might wish for.

What does she wish for?
Photo Credit: *UNHCR / H. Caux*

JOYCE CAROL OATES

THE SKY BLUE BALL

In a long-ago time when I didn't know *Yes I was happy, I was myself and I was happy.* In a long-ago time when I wasn't a child any longer yet wasn't entirely not-a-child. In a long-ago time when I seemed often to be alone, and imagined myself lonely. *Yet this is your truest self: alone, lonely.*

One day I found myself walking beside a high brick wall the color of dried blood, the aged bricks loose and moldering, and over the wall came flying a spherical object so brightly blue I thought it was a bird!—until it dropped a few yards in front of me, bouncing at a crooked angle off the broken sidewalk, and I saw that it was a rubber ball. A child had thrown a rubber ball over the wall, and I was expected to throw it back.

Hurriedly I let my things fall into the weeds, ran to snatch up the ball, which looked new, smelled new, spongy and resilient in my hand like a rubber ball I'd played with years before as a little girl; a ball I'd loved and had long ago misplaced; a ball I'd loved and had forgotten. "Here it comes!" I called, and tossed the ball back over the wall; I would have walked on except, a few seconds later, there came the ball again, flying back.

A game, I thought. *You can't quit a game.*

So I ran after the ball as it rolled in the road, in the gravelly dirt, and again snatched it up, squeezing it with pleasure, how spongy, how resilient a rubber ball, and again I tossed it over the wall; feeling happiness in swinging my arm as I hadn't done for years since I'd lost interest in such childish games. And this time I waited expectantly, and again it came!—the most beautiful sky blue rubber ball rising high, high into the air above my head and pausing for a heartbeat before it began to fall, to sink, like an object possessed of its own willful volition; so there was plenty of time for me to position myself beneath it and catch it firmly with both hands.

"Got it!"

I was fourteen years old and did not live in this neighborhood, nor anywhere in the town of Strykersville, New York (population 5,600). I lived on a small farm eleven miles to the north and I was brought to Strykersville by school bus, and consequently I was often alone; for this year, ninth grade, was my first at the school and I hadn't made many friends. And though I had relatives in Strykersville, these were not relatives close to my family; they were not relatives eager to acknowledge me; for we who still lived in the country, hadn't yet made the inevitable move into town, were perceived inferior to those who lived in town. And, in fact, my family was poorer than our relatives who lived in Strykersville.

At our school, teachers referred to the nine farm children bussed there as "North Country children." We were allowed to understand that "North Country children" differed significantly from Strykersville children.

I was not thinking of such things now, I was smiling thinking it must be a particularly playful child on the other side of the wall, a little girl like me; like the little girl I'd been; though the wall was ugly and forbidding, with rusted signs EMPIRE MACHINE PARTS and PRIVATE PROPERTY NO TRESPASSING. On the other side of the Chautauqua & Buffalo railroad yard was a street of small wood-frame houses; it must have been in one of these that the little girl, my invisible playmate, lived. She must be much younger than I was; for fourteen-year-old girls didn't play such heedless games with strangers, we grew up swiftly if our families were not well-to-do.

I threw the ball back over the wall, calling, "Hi! Hi, there!" But there was no reply. I waited; I was standing in broken concrete, amid a scrubby patch of weeds. Insects buzzed and droned around me as if in curiosity, yellow butterflies no larger than my smallest fingernail fluttered and caught in my hair, tickling me. The sun was bright as a nova in a pebbled-white soiled sky that was like a thin chamois cloth about to be lifted away and I thought, *This is the surprise I've been waiting for.* For somehow I had acquired the belief that a surprise, a nice surprise, was waiting for me. I had only to merit it, and it would happen. (And if I did not merit it, it would not happen.) Such a surprise could not come from God but only from strangers, by chance.

Another time the sky blue ball sailed over the wall, after a longer interval of perhaps thirty seconds; and at an unexpected angle, as if it had been thrown away from me, from my voice, purposefully. Yet there it came, as if it could not not come: my invisible playmate was obliged to continue the game. I had no hope of catching it but ran blindly into the road (which was partly asphalt and partly gravel and not much traveled except by trucks) and there came a dump truck headed at me, I heard the ugly shriek of brakes and a deafening angry horn and I'd fallen onto my knees, I'd cut my knees that were bare, probably I'd torn my skirt, scrambling quickly to my feet, my cheeks smarting with shame, for wasn't I too grown a girl for such behavior? "Get the hell out of the road!" a man's voice was furious in rectitude, the voice of so many adult men of my acquaintance, you did not question such voices, you did not doubt them, you ran quickly to get out of their way, already I'd snatched up the ball, panting like a dog, trying to hide the ball in my skirt as I turned, shrinking and ducking so the truck driver couldn't see my face, for what if he was someone who knew my father, what if he recognized me, knew my name. But already the truck was thundering past, already I'd been forgotten.

Back then I ran to the wall, though both my knees throbbed with pain, and I was shaking as if shivering, the air had grown cold, a shaft of cloud had pierced the sun. I threw the ball back over the wall again, underhand, so that it rose high, high—so that my invisible playmate would have plenty of time to run and catch it. And it disappeared behind the wall and I waited, I was breathing hard and did not investigate my bleeding knees, my torn skirt. More clouds pierced the sun and shadows moved swift and certain across the earth like predator fish. After a while I called out hesitantly, "Hi? Hello?" It was like a ringing

telephone you answer but no one is there. You wait, you in-
quire again, shyly, "Hello?" A vein throbbed in my forehead, a
tinge of pain glimmered behind my eyes, that warning of pain,
of punishment, following excitement. The child had drifted
away, I supposed; she'd lost interest in our game, if it was a
game. And suddenly it seemed silly and contemptible to me,
and sad: there I stood, fourteen years old, a long-limbed weed
of a girl, no longer a child yet panting and bleeding from the
knees, the palms of my hands, too, chafed and scraped and
dirty; there I stood alone in front of a moldering brick wall
waiting for—what?

It was my school notebook, my several textbooks I'd let fall
into the grass and I would afterward discover that my math
textbook was muddy, many pages damp and torn; my spiral
notebook in which I kept careful notes of the intransigent rules
of English grammar and sample sentences diagrammed was
soaked in a virulent-smelling chemical and my teacher's lauda-
tory comments in red and my grades of A (for all my grades at
Strykersville Junior High were A, of that I was obsessively
proud) had become illegible as if they were grades of C, D, F. I
should have taken up my books and walked hurriedly away and
put the sky blue ball out of my mind entirely but I was not so
free, through my life I've been made to realize that I am not
free, as others appear to be free, at all. For the "nice" surprise
carries with it the "bad" surprise and the two are intricately
entwined and they cannot be separated, nor even defined as
separate. So though my head pounded I felt obliged to look for
a way over the wall. Though my knees were scraped and bleeding I located a filthy oil drum and shoved it against the wall and

climbed shakily up on it, dirtying my hands and arms, my legs, my clothes, even more. And I hauled myself over the wall, and jumped down, a drop of about ten feet, the breath knocked out of me as I landed, the shock of the impact reverberating through me, along my spine, as if I'd been struck by a sledgehammer blow to the soles of my feet. At once I saw that there could be no little girl here, the factory yard was surely deserted, about the size of a baseball diamond totally walled in and overgrown with weeds pushing through cracked asphalt, thistles, stunted trees, and clouds of tiny yellow butterflies clustered here in such profusion I was made to see that they were not beautiful creatures but mere insects, horrible. And rushing at me as if my very breath sucked them at me, sticking against my sweaty face, and in my snarled hair.

Yet stubbornly I searched for the ball. I would not leave without the ball. I seemed to know that the ball must be there, somewhere on the other side of the wall, though the wall would have been insurmountable for a little girl. And at last, after long minutes of searching, in a heat of indignation I discovered the ball in a patch of chicory. It was no longer sky blue but faded and cracked; its dun-colored rubber showed through the venous-cracked surface, like my own ball, years ago. Yet I snatched it up in triumph, and squeezed it, and smelled it—it smelled of nothing: of the earth: of the sweating palm of my own hand.

EDITOR'S NOTE

This book was created to raise funds to establish libraries in refugee camps in eastern Chad, home to a quarter of a million refugees from neighboring Darfur. Some of the world's best-selling and most honored authors and poets have contributed their work free of charge so that as much of the book's proceeds as possible can benefit the refugees. Yet nowhere in their work will you read the word *Darfur.* Instead, these stories and poems are about wishes. What is the connection?

Darfur is a word that has become associated with genocide, one of the worst evils of mankind. Like *Rwanda* or *Holocaust,* it conjures images of war—but more than war, of extreme bru-tality aimed at destroying an ethnic group. Three hundred thousand people dead. At least two and a half million forced from their homes. Over 3,300 villages destroyed or damaged. Unknown thousands of women and children raped and tor-tured. This suffering is incomprehensible to most of the world. Even though we want to help, it can be difficult to understand how. What could the people of Darfur wish for that we could actually provide?

In 2003, when the war began, what they wanted was a greater role in their own destiny, in the political and economic life of Darfur. Darfur is a California-sized region of the largest country in Africa, Sudan. It was home to roughly six million people, but they had little say in their own governance. The Sudanese government largely excluded the indigenous ethnic groups of Darfur from decision making. So, in February and March of 2003, after years of being marginalized, two groups of Darfuris, the Sudan Liberation Army and the Justice and Equality Movement, rebelled against the central government. The Sudanese government responded with what the United States, the International Criminal Court, and many others have called genocide. They did not merely fight the rebels; they targeted civilians from the tribes that most supported the rebels. Targeted for annihilation. Using Sudan's military, and arming rival ethnic groups to form militias called Janjaweed, they burned villages to the ground and terrorized with massacres and sexual violence. Nobody was safe in Darfur, not even the youngest children.

By the end of 2003, 100,000 Darfuris, fearing for their lives in Sudan, had fled across the border into the country of Chad. In doing so, they officially became refugees, people who live outside their home country because they are afraid to return. They are still there. The UN Refugee Agency, UNHCR, responded to protect these extremely vulnerable people arriving in Chad, one of the least developed countries in the world. They built basic facilities to provide food, water, shelter, medicine, and security in a harsh desert. At first, the top priority of the emergency was just keeping the refugees alive, and doing so strained the resources the international community could muster.

But as UNICEF Goodwill Ambassador Mia Farrow's Foreword to this book reveals, even people who are struggling to stay alive and have suffered terrible tragedies have wishes for their future. The young refugee in the Foreword wants to be a doctor and is desperate for the education he knows is his best hope to make that dream come true. He is not alone. Of the 259,162 refugees living in the twelve camps in eastern Chad as of September 2010, 62 percent were under the age of eighteen, and most of them under twelve. The camps are young, filled with 100,000 or more school-age children.

The host country of Chad cannot educate the refugees. By the time most of us have entered the third grade, we have already received more education than the average Chadian adult has in his entire life. So, whatever education these children would receive would have to be provided by UNHCR, in addition to basic lifesaving assistance. With a very limited budget, however, education could not initially be a top priority.

Now, in 2011, there is a greater focus on educating the refugees. Even though international funding is still inadequate, priorities are shifting from emergency response to long-term care. Partly this is because of the stark realization that, eight years into what has been called the world's worst humanitarian crisis, there are still no prospects the refugees will return home.

Some of the reasons it is important to educate the refugees are obvious, and mirror the "stay in school" messages common in the developed world, but others might surprise. UNHCR has said that "education has assumed a critical importance in protecting youth from forced recruitment" by militias active in and around the refugee camps and in protecting girls from very early marriages. Keeping children in school also helps to prevent their abuse as laborers. And thinking about the roots of the crisis, it makes sense that Darfuris particularly want their children to be educated so they can be stronger leaders for Darfur, if they eventually return.

Most primary-school-age refugees are now attending classes in the camps, even if the school facilities are profoundly basic and still inadequate. For older students, though, there are very few opportunities. Where school buildings cannot support the number of students, classes sometimes meet outside on the desert sand in scorching temperatures well over 100 degrees Fahrenheit. The refugees are eager students. Some have even returned to Darfur, risking their lives, to take graduation exams that will be recognized by the Sudanese government. However, even the strongest desire to learn cannot overcome two basic obstacles facing education in the camps: lack of textbooks and lack of teachers with advanced knowledge. These are areas where our libraries can help.

Without textbooks, and with teachers who might be only a few years more advanced than their students, where can refugee students turn for knowledge? Not the Internet and not television, which they also do not have. A library, containing books on exactly the subjects they are trying to learn, is a practical answer. It can also be a major tool for training teachers, who can share the information contained in library books with their many students.

Helping to educate refugees is a way to fight against the

hopelessness of a historic crisis. What has happened in Darfur has caused them to lose so much—their homes, their families, their livelihoods, their health—and even in Chad many have continued to be victimized. In this climate of insecurity, education is one of the few things we can give to refugees that can never be taken away. It is always a step forward, toward their dreams for the future.

Libraries will do much to aid the refugees' education, especially beyond primary school, but that is not all they can do. If you have ever felt sad and opened a book to escape into another world, you know that reading can have emotional benefits. Imagine how great the need for escape is for the victims of genocide. Many refugee children and women are suffering from deep psychological wounds. Surely they deserve as much as anyone else to enjoy the simple pleasures of reading, if only to experience for precious moments lives that are a little happier.

We cannot say that libraries will resolve the crisis in Darfur or fulfill the wishes of an entire people to return to their homeland, to rebuild, and to live in peace. But each book contains within its pages the possibility of making some refugee's wishes come true. It might be a book that sets a young student on the path to being the first doctor to return to his village in Darfur. It might be a book that teaches a new trade to support a family. Or it might be a book that allows a mother to see her child experience a normal childhood, if only while reading.

All of the supporters of this book are helping to bring those books to the people of Darfur. When you read on these pages a story or a poem about wishes, think about the wishes of the refugees.

Book Wish Foundation, an all-volunteer 501(c)(3) public charity based in Reston, Virginia, USA, has organized this book and will donate 100 percent of the proceeds it receives to UNHCR to establish libraries in Darfuri refugee camps in eastern Chad. To track the progress of the libraries, to learn more about the Darfur crisis, and to take other actions to aid the refugees, please visit www.bookwish.org and www.unhcr.org.

Logan Kleinwaks,
Co-Founder, Book Wish Foundation
January 25, 2011

SELECTED ONLINE RESOURCES
MORE AT BOOKWISH.ORG

unhcr.org/darfur
UNHCR's current activities and strategy for helping refugees in Chad

ushmm.org/maps/projects/darfur
Satellite imagery and mapping showing the destruction of villages in Darfur

twitter.com/refugees
UNHCR's Twitter stream, a daily source for news about refugees

unhcr.org/convention
International treaties that define and provide legal protection for refugees

miafarrow.org
UNICEF Goodwill Ambassador Mia Farrow's blog about Darfur and other crises

darfurdreamteam.org
A program connecting U.S. schools with students in Darfuri refugee camps

unhcr.org/refworld
Up-to-date reports from many sources related to refugee situations around the world

un.org/en/documents/udhr
The Universal Declaration of Human Rights, including the right to education (Article 26)

THE AUTHORS

MEG CABOT Her best-known series, *The Princess Diaries*, has been published in over 38 countries, winning awards from the American Library Association (Best Books for Young Adults) and a spot on the BBC's list of the UK's "100 best-loved novels." She has written more than 50 books, such as *Airhead*, *Abandon*, *The Mediator*, and the Allie Finkle's Rules for Girls series. Author of romance, comedy, and the paranormal, she has contributed writing for many charitable causes.

JEANNE DuPRAU Best known for her post-apocalyptic series The Books of Ember, of which the first book, *The City of Ember*, was an American Library Association Notable Book for Children, she is also the author of nonfiction works on such diverse topics as adoption, cloning, and Zen meditation. She has been an English teacher, a writing teacher, an editor, and a technical writer for Apple Computer.

NIKKI GIOVANNI One of America's most widely read poets, an Oprah Winfrey "Living Legend," NAACP Image Award winner, and the first to receive the Rosa L. Parks Woman of Courage Award. Author of over 30 books of poetry, children's books, essays, and a Grammy-finalist poetry album. A prominent voice in the "Black Arts Movement" of the

1960s/70s, she is a distinguished English professor at Virginia Tech and recipient of more than twenty honorary degrees.

JOHN GREEN The *New York Times* bestselling author of *Looking for Alaska*, *An Abundance of Katherines*, and *Paper Towns*. He is also the coauthor, with David Levithan, of *Will Grayson, Will Grayson*. He was 2006 recipient of the Michael L. Printz Award, a 2009 Edgar Award winner, and has twice been a finalist for the Los Angeles Times Book Prize. Green's books have been published in more than a dozen languages.

CORNELIA FUNKE The world's bestselling book author in the German language, she was one of *Time* magazine's 100 Most Influential People in 2005. Her Inkworld trilogy and other books have sold over 100 million copies. *Reckless*, the first in a new series, is based on her extensive knowledge of central European folktales. Formerly a social worker helping children from difficult backgrounds and a children's book illustrator, she supports charities that help refugees, victims of torture, and sick and abused children.

KAREN HESSE The winner of a Newbery Medal for *Out of the Dust*, a free-verse novel set during the Dust Bowl era, she often tackles difficult historical subjects in her books for young readers, such as the Ku Klux Klan (*Witness*), the Holocaust (*The Cats in Krasinski Square*), nuclear disaster (*Phoenix Rising*), and the challenges faced by immigrants (*Letters from Rifka*). In 2002, she was awarded a prestigious MacArthur Fellowship.

ANN M. MARTIN Her series, The Baby-sitter's Club, is one of the most successful of all time, having sold more than 175 million copies and spawned many spin-offs. A long-awaited prequel, *The Summer Before*, was published in 2010. She is the author of many standalone novels, including *Everything for a Dog*, *Belle Teal*, and the Newbery Honor–winning *A Corner of the Universe*, and is the co-author of the *Doll People* books. Charities she founded, The Lisa Libraries and the Ann M. Martin Foundation, benefit children, arts, education, literacy, and stray and abused animals.

ALEXANDER McCALL SMITH Author of over 80 books, including five ongoing series, most notably The No. 1 Ladies' Detective Agency novels, which are set in Botswana. His books have been translated into 46 languages and he has been the recipient of numerous awards throughout the world. He was previously Professor of Medical Law at the University of Edinburgh but now devotes his time to writing.

MARILYN NELSON While Poet Laureate of Connecticut (2001–2006), she founded Soul Mountain Retreat to assist poets from racially or culturally underrepresented groups. A three-time National Book Award finalist (*The Homeplace*, *The Fields of Praise: New And Selected Poems*, *Carver: A Life in Poems*), Newbery Honor winner (*Carver: A Life In Poems*), and author or translator of over 12 books for young adults and children, she is a professor emerita at the University of Connecticut.

NAOMI SHIHAB NYE Elected a Chancellor of the Academy of American Poets in 2010, she is author or editor of 30 books, including the National Book Award finalist *19 Varieties of Gazelle: Poems of the Middle East* and the Arab American Book Award winner *Honeybee: Poems and Short Prose*. Her work often draws on her Palestinian-American heritage and intercultural experiences. As the daughter of a refugee, she advocates in many schools internationally for human rights, freedom of expression, and dialogue, instead of war.

JOYCE CAROL OATES A Distinguished Professor of Humanities at Princeton University, where she has taught creative writing since 1978, she is among the most prominent and prolific American authors, known especially for her Gothic fiction and social realism. Winner of a National Book Award (*them*), multiple Pulitzer Prize finalist (*Blonde, Black Water, What I Lived For*), master of the short story (two O. Henry Awards, PEN/Malamud Award), noted essayist, poet, and playwright, her more than 56 novels and 32 short story collections include such works for young adults as *Freaky Green Eyes, Small Avalanches and Other Stories*, and *Big Mouth & Ugly Girl*.

NATE POWELL Graphic novelist whose *Swallow Me Whole* won the Eisner Award for Best Original Graphic Novel, the Ignatz Award for Outstanding Artist, and was a Los Angeles Times Book Prize finalist—the first graphic novel to be nominated for the prize in almost 20 years. Also a musician, manager of Harlan Records, and illustrator for record labels, he worked for a decade helping adults with developmental disabilities.

SOFIA QUINTERO Called one of the New School of Activists Most Likely to Change New York by *City Lights Magazine*, she writes with gritty realism about social issues surrounding race, class, gender, and hip hop culture. Her debut novel for young adults, *Efrain's Secret*, chronicles an inner-city teen's extreme plan to make it into an Ivy League school. She also writes under the name Black Artemis, and co-founded a multimedia production company that produces socially conscious entertainment.

GARY SOTO Recipient of the Hispanic Heritage Foundation's Literature Award and a National Book Award finalist for his poetry, his work has appeared in over 30 million textbooks. His more than 35 books of poetry, fiction, and short stories include vivid depictions of Mexican-American life. The Gary Soto Literary Museum at Fresno City College houses his writings.

R. L. STINE With more than 300 million books sold, he is among the bestselling authors of all time. His *Goosebumps* series made the *Guinness Book of World Records*, and *USA Today* named him America's #1 bestselling author three years in a row. Among his many other works is the top teen horror series, *Fear Street*. A three-time winner of both the Nickelodeon and Disney Adventures Kids' Choice Awards, he has contributed to and edited anthologies for many charitable causes.

FRANCISCO X. STORK His debut novel, *The Way of the Jaguar*, was a recipient of the Chicano/Latino Literary Prize. He is also the author of three young adult novels, *Behind the*

Eyes, *Marcelo in the Real World* (recipient of the ALA's Schneider Family Award), and *The Last Summer of the Death Warriors*. He currently works as an attorney for a state agency that develops affordable housing.

CYNTHIA VOIGT Books from her Tillerman Cycle series have received prestigious awards including the Newbery Medal (*Dicey's Song*), Newbery Honor (*A Solitary Blue*), and German Youth Literature Prize (*The Runner*). In these, other series such as *Bad Girls*, and many standalone books for teens and middle-graders, she writes about serious issues such as child abandonment and racism, as well as mystery and fantasy. For her lasting contributions to literature for young adults, she received the Margaret A. Edwards Award in 1995.

JANE YOLEN Called "America's Hans Christian Andersen" (*Newsweek*) and the "Aesop of the 20th century" (*New York Times*) for her children's fantasy, folklore, and science fiction stories. She has written over 300 books for all ages, including more than 175 children's picture books, 31 poetry collections, novels, chapter books, songbooks, essays, and plays. Her honors include a Caldecott Medal for *Owl Moon*, two Nebula Awards for short stories ("Sister Emily's Lightship" and "Lost Girls"), two Christopher Medals, and the World Fantasy Award.

ACKNOWLEDGMENTS

This book is an expression of many people's desire to help refugees from Darfur. We have the utmost respect and appreciation for: the authors and poets who shared their valuable talent freely for this cause; Mia Farrow, an advocate without limits, who contributed an important personal link to the refugees; our literary agent, Brenda Bowen, who donated her essential guidance pro bono; and especially the team at Penguin/G. P. Putnam's Sons for using the strength of a publishing industry titan to lift up some of the world's neediest readers. Without Nancy Paulsen, Susan Kochan, and our tireless editor, Stacey Barney, who supported and nurtured our vision, this book would not be possible.

We owe a special gratitude to Alexander McCall Smith for being the first author to commit to this project, when it was nothing but an idea; to Cornelia Funke and Ann M. Martin for joining even before we had a publisher; and to the team at

UNHCR, especially Greg Millar, for their invaluable collaboration to help maximize the aid we can give to the Darfuris.

Critical assistance was provided by David Axelrod, Faye Bender, Amy Berkower, Candice Bradley, Regina Brooks, Eliza Fischer, Prof. Virginia Fowler, Gina Gagliano, Nancy Gallt, Leila Gordon, Julianne Hancock, Elizabeth Harding, Rebecca Hearn, Merrilee Heifetz, Susan Knopf, Oliver Latsch, Kendra Marcus, Steve Rosato, Susanne Rudloff, Robin Straus, and Lesley Winton. We are most grateful to them personally and for the generosity of SirsiDynix, HarperCollins, Verlag Friedrich Oetinger, BookExpo America, the London Book Fair, and the Frankfurt Book Fair.

Thank you all for working together with us to make some of the refugees' wishes come true.

With gratitude to all who have joined the authors and poets by supporting or inspiring support for the refugee camp libraries:

Pam Omidyar
Cassandra and Vernon S.
The Lane Family and Girl Scout Troop 5712

Christian Boutte • Kingston L. Brunson • Janice L. Wilkins

Edward Abbott • Stephanie Abbott • Deborah A. Allan • Merri Ann Allan • Patricia Robertson Amusa Shonubi • Kaitlyn D. B. • Siomara Joia Baluarte • Cole Eugene Barnes • Kameron Edward Barnes • Tyler Michael Barnes • Chus Bello • Majida Ben Jemaa • Munir Ben Jemaa • Ida Bentsen • Coleen Binshtok • Martha Sumrall Boshnick • Alex Brooks • Hannah Brooks • Curtis Brown, Ltd. • Carl Brunson • Jill Brunson • Paul Brunson • Rachel Kramer Bussel • Thomas Carroll • Kathy Casey • Aurelia Castillo • Candice Chiu • Ratinan Choochaimangkhala • Edmund

Chow • Daniel West Cohen • Karen Cushman • Leah Cushman • Hanis D. • Darfur and Beyond • Wyatt West Dean • Eden Amelia Ewell • Everett Neal Ewell • Grayson Michael Ewell • Arielle R. Feller • Micah B. Feller • Eric Ferguson • Juan A. Fernandez • Donald Fischer • Emily Fischer • Jason Fischer • Wendy Fischer • Shea Foley • Dale Friedman • Nancy Gallt • Farah Géhy • Pamela Goldberg • Leila Gordon • Remington M. Gray • Riley Hope Grayson • Mrs. Heise • Samantha Leigh Hendy • Kira Thomasdotter Ingo • Stella Thomasdotter Ingo • Monica Itzel • Louise Jacob • Abraham Phillips Jaspen • Anne Pruitt Jaspen • Leo Broughton Jaspen • David Johnson • Doni Kay • Rebecca Kennedy • Jonathan Kleinwaks • Alvina L. • Angie M. L. • Julia Gelfand Lang • Laura Langlie • Chris Lanphere • Ann Larson • Kristin Levine • Kelly Starling Lyons • Jacob Males • Clare Mansfield • Mary Jo Marchant • Dora Marcus • Claire Mayerick • Erin Mazursky • Aroha Millar • Frankie Millar • Jacqueline Mitchell • Patricia Mounsey • Allan Nelkin • Melanie Nelkin • Sheila O'Connor • Hannah P. • Julia P. • Shaela P. • Sasha Parsons • Betty Puszakowski • Ethan Amelia R. • Laura Register • Nikisha Riley • Mariam S. • Sekou S. • Maxine Schmidt • Adam Schupack • Rachel Schupack • Danny Sedlazek • Sue Sedlazek • Walt Sedlazek • Elizabeth Shaw • Emily Shaw • Abby Simon • Alan Sitomer • Adeline Claudia Sozanski • Gilda Squire • Rebecca Stanley • Danielle Stark • Joanne K. Stathos • Kerry Stubbs • Judy

Swanson • Chris Sylvester • Don Sylvester • Laurie Thompson • Aunt Trish • Danette Vigilante • West Family • Benjamin Wexler • Joanna Whitehead • Cory Williams • Darcy Wishard • Larry Yungk

Past contributors to Book Wish Foundation have also significantly advanced this cause. Thank you!